A Cassandra Mystery™

TREASURE BEACH

BY JENNIFER AUSTIN

ILLUSTRATED BY ANN MEISEL

A BYRON PREISS BOOK

PUBLISHERS • GROSSET & DUNLAP • NEW YORK
A MEMBER OF THE PUTNAM PUBLISHING GROUP

Library of Congress Catalog Card Number: 89-84102

ISBN 0-448-37703-9

A B C D E F G H I J

Special thanks to Barbara Steiner

Cover painting by Ann Meisel
Book design by Alex Jay/Studio J

"**L**ook at that!" said Cassie, pointing to a gold medallion set with huge emeralds. "Imagine wearing something that beautiful on a chain around your neck." Her amber eyes sparkled as she pushed back the honey-blond hair that had fallen over her face.

"I like the rosary with the red coral and gold beads." Gran bent over the glass of the display case to read the exhibit label. "This says it's one of the most stunning artifacts ever recovered from a shipwreck."

Cassie B. Jones, her sister Melanie, and their grandmother had come to the museum in Cleveland to see the exhibit called "Treasures of the Deep." Most of the treasure had been recovered from the wreck of the Spanish galleon *Atocha*, one of the

1

richest treasure ships ever found off the coast of Florida.

"You guys can have all that jewelry," said ten-year-old Melanie, pushing up her horn-rimmed glasses, which were always sliding down her nose. She was peering into the next case. "I'll take this." She pointed to a pile of gold doubloons.

"That figures, Mel," said Cassie when she and Gran had moved over to take a look. "And what would you do with so much money?"

"I'd run away to Hollywood to see all my favorite stars," answered Mel, sighing. "You always get to go some place, Cassie, and I never go anywhere."

"You got to come to Cleveland today," Cassie pointed out.

"Oh, that doesn't count." Melanie gave Cassie a disgusted look and moved on to the next case.

Cassie understood what Mel meant. Cleveland, Ohio, was a far cry from the exotic places Cassie had visited with her British pen pal, Alexandra Bennett. Alex was a beautiful debutante whose father, Lloyd Bennett, was the publisher of a leading British newspaper.

When Cassie had begun writing to Alex more than three years ago, she'd signed her name Cassandra Best. Cassandra Best Jones was Cassie's full name, but no one in her small Ohio hometown called her anything but Cassie. Cassandra Best sounded like the kind of exciting, sophisticated girl Cassie had always wanted to be. It had been as Cassandra Best that Cassie had first gone to England to meet Alex. While there, she had saved her friend from a deadly kidnapping scheme and established her own reputation as a daring detective. And so Cassandra Best, detective, was born.

Now whenever Alex ran across a mystery in her travels as society columnist for her father's newspaper, she called on her pen pal for help. And Cassie, no matter what she was doing at the time, would travel any distance to solve the case.

The question is, mused the eighteen-year-old detective, where in the world will I go next?

"Come and see this," called Mel, rousing Cassie from her reverie. Mel stood in front of a pile of gold bars. There was a small sign in front of the display that read:

After Columbus discovered the New World in 1492, the riches of her colonies helped make Spain the most powerful nation in history. From 1530 to 1800, six to eight billion dollars worth of gold and silver were mined in Spanish American colonies and shipped to Spain. That wealth changed the course of European history.

"Just a fraction of that much gold would change my history," said Cassie, laughing. "Can you imagine finding all this on the ocean floor?'' She spread her arms wide to include the whole collection.

"The ocean's a big place. It's a wonder any of this has ever been found,'' remarked Gran.

"The label says the *Atocha* sank in a storm in 1622 and wasn't discovered until 1985,'' said Cassie. "And it took the treasure hunter sixteen years to find it.''

"This is sure a great exhibit,'' said Mel, sighing. "But I've had enough history for today. Can we have those ice cream sundaes you promised, Gran?''

"Okay, okay.'' Gran laughed and looked at Mel. "Oh, to be so skinny.''

"Willowy, Gran,'' Mel said, prancing away. "Willowy.''

Cassie and Gran laughed again. Cassie loved being with her grandmother, who had a wonderful sense of humor. Only Gran knew the whole story of Cassie B. Jones's double life as detective Cassandra Best. Cassie knew she could always tell Gran all the details of her adventures, no matter how dangerous. Gran had had her own adventures as a nurse in England during World War II, and had always kept her youthful spirit.

In the car on the way home to Milltown, Gran asked, "Have you heard from Alex recently, Cassie?''

Cassie thought of her glamorous friend, Alexandra. "No, I haven't heard from her for a couple of

4

weeks," she answered. "I don't even know where she is right now." Cassie had trouble keeping track of Alex's busy schedule.

"She'll call you from Paris or Rome or Hawaii—someplace exotic. She goes to the most *won*derful places," groaned Mel.

It was usually Alex's work that took her abroad, but she and her father had friends and social connections all over the world.

Cassie hoped that wherever Alex was, she'd find that she needed Cassandra Best on a job.

"Wishing a little detective work would come your way?" asked Gran with a smile. Mel had bounced out of the car the minute Cassie pulled into the driveway, leaving the two alone.

"You can always read my mind, Gran." Cassie smiled at her understanding grandmother. "After a case, it's hard to come home to being just plain Cassie Jones."

"You will never, by any stretch of the imagination, be plain," said Gran, patting her granddaughter fondly on the cheek. "I would have given anything for lovely blond hair like yours when I was a girl." She got out of the car and followed Mel into the house.

Cassie smiled at the compliment and drove the car into the garage. It wasn't her looks she was thinking of. She wanted another chance to be daring detective Cassandra Best. Most of all, she wanted to solve another mystery.

After dinner, Cassie helped her mother clear the table while the rest of the family gathered in the living room to watch a favorite TV program. Cassie was just debating whether to join them or go up to her room to read when the phone rang.

"I'll get it," she said, dashing into the hall. Maybe it was Alex at last.

Was she developing a psychic connection all the way to England? "Alex," Cassie said in delight. "How are you? What's happening?"

"Oh, not much." Alex's voice was teasing.

"Alexandra Bennett, don't try to fool me," Cassie said sternly. "Where are you?"

"Well, I'm in Florida. It's extraordinarily hot here, and there's nothing to do but lie around on the beach."

"Oh, you poor thing!" Cassie joked. "What are you doing in Florida?"

"I have an aunt here," Alex explained. "My father's sister, Owena, ran away to America when she was young to follow her true love. Isn't that romantic?"

"It's a wonderful story," agreed Cassie. "So they live in Florida?"

"Well, my uncle died years ago. Now Aunt Owena lives alone in the house they built in the Keys."

"Any particular reason for your visit?" asked Cassie.

"Yes, she's giving a party," said Alex. Cassie laughed, and Alex explained further. "My uncle was quite a knowledgeable amateur archaeologist. Since his death, Owena has devoted all her time to the Key West Archaeological Foundation that he set up. The gala will benefit the foundation, and it's going to be a fabulous party. People from all over the world are going to be there. So when Owena called and invited Daddy and me, he asked me to write an article on the gala and the foundation for the newspaper."

"It sounds like a lot of fun," said Cassie. Had Alex called to invite her to the party? she wondered, her excitement growing.

"To make a long story short, Cassie, how would you like to come to Key West?"

"Oh, I'd love to, Alex—but I hope I won't be expected to donate to the foundation, too?"

"No, silly." Alex laughed. "Actually, this is business."

"Business! Is this a case?" Cassie whispered the question, in case anyone was listening.

"I thought you'd never ask." Alex lowered her voice conspiratorially. "Something very odd is going on here."

"What do you mean, odd?"

"It's a long story. One of Owena's oldest friends, Whit Bromfield, is a treasure hunter."

"Treasure! What kind of treasure?" asked Cassie.

"Sunken treasure. Whit's looking for a treasure ship that went down off the cost of Florida in the sixteenth century. Owena's foundation is helping finance Whit's expedition."

"This is incredible, Alex. I just saw a treasure exhibit in Cleveland today. But tell me what you think is odd," urged Cassie.

"Whit's had a lot of bad luck lately," said Alex. "One of his ships vanished without a trace. And last month one of his divers disappeared in a storm."

"Maybe sharks, or . . ." Cassie's mind was already clicking along.

"I haven't finished yet," Alex warned. "Besides that, equipment has been damaged and some divers injured. So much has happened that Whit's decided it's not just bad luck. He thinks someone's trying to keep him from finding the treasure ship.

"I told Whit and Owena about my friend, Cassandra Best, the detective. And Owena thinks it would be a sound investment of the foundation's funds to send you a plane ticket to Key West immediately."

"Immediately?" Cassie took a deep breath.

"Well, tomorrow is soon enough," Alex said with a laugh. "Throw a few bathing suits into your suitcase and head for the airport. A ticket with your name on it will be waiting for you."

"Sounds great," said Cassie. She could hardly contain her excitement. "I'll have to check with my parents, but they're sure to say yes."

"I can hardly wait to see you tomorrow, Cassie," Alex said, a note of affection in her voice. "I've missed you."

"Same here, Alex."

Cassie hung up the phone and let out a whoop of joy. Treasure-hunting! Never in her wildest dreams had she thought she'd ever have the chance to look for sunken treasure.

She practically floated back into the living room.

"What was that all about?" her mother asked, turning down the sound on the television.

"And why were you whispering?" Mel ran over to Cassie, her pigtails bouncing up and down.

"I wasn't whispering," said Cassie. "And if I was, it's because some people in this house are much too nosy." Cassie grabbed her younger sister and hugged her. "Meaning you, Melanie."

"I'm nosy, too," her father said. "Was that Alex?"

"Yes. She called to invite me to Florida. She's visiting her aunt down in Key West. She's already called the airport to reserve a plane ticket for me."

"What about your job?" asked her mother. Cassie worked at the Milltown Mystery Playhouse, doing production work and acting in the occasional bit part. She hoped to be an actress someday.

"Mom, I was on construction for this show. Now that the set is up, I have a few days off before the next project begins. No one will even miss me."

Gran finally spoke. "An actress needs to be a student of human nature. When better to study people than while traveling? Cassie may not always have this opportunity."

Cassie smiled appreciatively at her grandmother. Her father nodded his permission, and her mother said, "Just get a tan for me, Cassie. It's been a long time since I had a week at the beach."

"I'd better go pack if I'm going to leave tomorrow," Cassie said. It was time to escape to her room.

Mel followed her. "You're going off to meet dozens of handsome guys on the beach. And I have to stay here and deal with fifth-grade boys." She made a rude noise and stuck out her tongue while holding her nose. Then she flopped on Cassie's bed to watch Cassie pack.

Cassie suspected that more important things waited for her in Florida than boywatching. She felt more than ready to meet whatever came her way.

Good-bye Milltown, hello adventure!

*L*ate the next morning Cassie walked through the crowds in the busy Miami airport. So many people around her were speaking other languages, she almost felt as if she had flown out of the country.

She shouldered her denim duffel, pleased at how light it was. Lightweight packing was a skill she was practicing. No matter where she was, she wanted to be able to take off at a moment's notice.

She finally found the departure gate for her connection to Key West, and for a few minutes she concentrated on watching people. She wondered if she could spot a criminal if she saw him. What about that shifty-eyed man with two tennis rackets and the suspicious-looking bulge in his jacket pocket? Or the plump woman with the two Pekingese dogs? The dogs would be a great cover. She could slip drugs or jewels or whatever into their carrying cases. . . .

Oh stop it, Cassie, she scolded herself. You've been watching too much TV.

Her flight was announced and Cassie boarded her plane. It was a short flight. When she landed in Key West, she hurried into the waiting area and looked around for a familiar face.

"Cassie!" Finally she heard Alex shouting her name.

Cassie turned and saw Alex rush up to her.

"Oh, Cassie, I could hardly wait to see you. You look great!" Alex gave her a hug.

"Alex!" Cassie hugged her back. "You look pretty wonderful yourself."

Wonderful was an understatement. Alex's hair flowed around her shoulders in dark waves touched with copper. Her chic, bright blue outfit made her eyes look even bluer, and she had the peaches-and-cream complexion that only English girls seem to inherit. Gold clips glittered on her ears. She wore a wide bracelet on the same wrist as her gold diamond-studded watch.

Cassie knew she could never compete with Alex's wardrobe, but clothes had never been important to her except as costumes.

"Do you have all your baggage?" Alex asked. When Cassie nodded yes, Alex grabbed her arm and said, "Come on then, hurry. I asked the cab driver to wait. I didn't want to lose him."

Tugged by Alex, Cassie practically ran to the taxi stand. The young taxi driver gave the two girls a big smile and tucked them into the backseat of his cab.

"Tell me everything that's happened to you since I saw you last," demanded Cassie. She decided to wait until later to ask about the mystery.

"That'll take weeks," said Alex, laughing.

She launched into a recital of the doings of London's rich and famous. Not for the first time, Cassie marveled at the people Alex knew.

While her friend talked, Cassie glanced out the windows of the cab at the fashionable resort city of Key West. Everywhere was lush, tropical vegetation—palm trees, hibiscus, and lovely pink-and-red bushes of bougainvillaea. Many of the older homes were gray and weathered, looking as if they might belong in a New England seacoast town. As they drove past one beach, Cassie noticed people were surfing.

"I didn't know you could surf here," said Cassie.

"Yes," answered the cabbie. "It takes a storm to get really big waves, but we like to claim we have every water sport there is. Do you surf?"

"No, but I'd like to try it," said Cassie.

"Here's the marina, ladies," the driver announced a few minutes later. The girls hopped out and Alex paid him.

"There's Keir Gardner," Alex said, pointing to a very tan and handsome young man who stood in a motorboat tied to the dock. He looked about eighteen, and he wore ragged jeans, worn loafers, and an orange patterned shirt. Half a doubloon dangled from a chain around his neck. "Keir's mother is Aunt Owena's companion and housekeeper."

Keir gave Cassie a big smile when Alex introduced her. "Welcome to the Keys, Cassandra. Is this your first trip to Florida?"

"Yes," answered Cassie, mesmerized by Keir's eyes. They were so dark brown, they looked almost black.

Keir Gardner took Cassie's duffel and stowed it away on the outboard cruiser. Then he took her hand and helped her step on board, holding her steady until she got her balance and was seated. Alex followed a bit more gracefully.

"How big is the key that Aunt Owena lives on?" Cassie asked Alex when they were both seated.

"Sand Dollar Key isn't very big, but she owns half of it. Whit Bromfield owns the other half. And wait until you see Aunt Owena's house. It's like a Southern mansion from *Gone With the Wind*."

Cassie couldn't imagine owning part of an island. She straightened her shoulders and tossed her head back, letting the breeze blow her long blond hair out of her eyes. Keir steered the boat skillfully, skimming it across the clear blue waters off Key West.

Hugging her knees, Cassie tried to conceal her excitement. Yesterday Ohio. Today a tropical island in the Florida Keys. What more could she ask for? She didn't care how big the island was.

It was late afternoon by the time they neared the island. As they tied up at the dock, Cassie looked up and down the coastline. The beach was very narrow but covered with sand so white it looked like snow. About seventy-five feet up the beach, an impenetrable tangle of bushes and mangrove trees met the sand.

"It's really just a movie set," joked Alex, snatching up her purse while Cassie took in the scene.

Cassie laughed. The island *did* look like a set right out of *Key Largo*, one of Cassie's favorite old movies. She could almost see Humphrey Bogart and Lauren Bacall coming down to meet them on the deserted beach.

Keir helped them from the cruiser, handed Cassie her bag, then got back on the boat. "I'll see you later," he said. "I've got a few chores to do here."

Alex located a trail, just wide enough for one, in the thick bush. Falling in behind Alex, Cassie trudged uphill on the narrow path, which was covered with crushed white oyster shells. All she could hear was the crunch of feet on shell and the occasional screech of a bird.

Alex turned around and grinned at Cassie. "Are

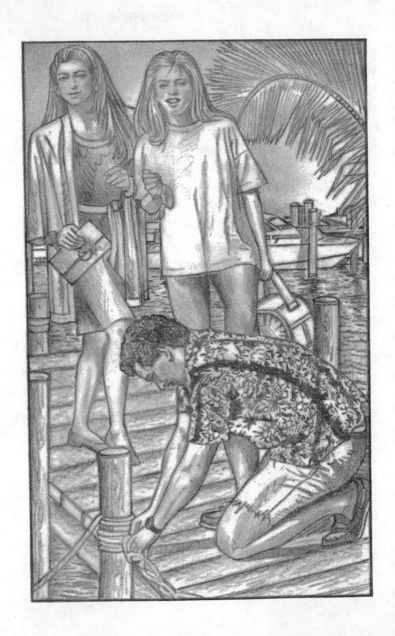

you ready?'' she asked, as if she had a surprise in store. And she did.

The trail led to a clearing where massive trees dripped with Spanish moss. They looked like old men with shaggy gray-green beards. A thick lawn, lush and green, cushioned their steps like expensive carpet. And ahead, in a pool of sunlight, stood a real Southern mansion.

''Look at all those porches,'' said Cassie, gazing in awe at the scene before her. The stately home was surrounded by elaborate gardens full of bright tropical flowers. For a moment, Cassie forgot her real reason for coming to the Keys. How could anything ''odd'' happen in such an idyllic place?

''Those aren't porches, Cassie, they're verandas,'' Alex reminded her.

''Well, pardon me, Miss Alex.'' Cassie put on a deep Southern accent. ''I declare, this is one of the most *bee*-utiful homes I have ever seen.''

''Aunt Owena is at a lawn party in town,'' said Alex, opening the huge, ornately carved front door of the house for Cassie. ''But she said to make ourselves at home. Whit will be joining us for dinner, and I know you'll want to ask him some questions.''

''I certainly will,'' said Cassie.

They walked down the long hall which led to the back of the house. The rooms were high-ceilinged, furnished with Casablanca fans and wicker furniture. Antiques and archaeological pieces salvaged from shipwrecks appeared everywhere. Huge bouquets of fresh flowers provided spots of color on every table and desk.

Tucked away almost under the stairs was a doorway that led to what Alex called the "green room."

"Oh, how charming." The view from the doorway took Cassie's breath away.

The room was really a glassed-in veranda, with sunlight streaming in on three sides. The floor was checkered in shades of light-green flagstone. Along one wall ran a white wicker couch covered with green-and-white patterned chintz. A light-green wicker chaise lounge sat opposite. House plants—spiders, philodendrons, ferns, and palms—sat or hung everywhere. The room looked like a very fancy greenhouse.

"I like to have my afternoon tea here," said Alex. "In fact, I could use a spot of tea right now—unless you'd rather go swimming." Alex looked at her watch. "Well, perhaps there's time for both, since Aunt Owena serves a late dinner."

"I can hardly wait to jump into the ocean," said Cassie.

"There's also a huge pool." Alex led the way upstairs. "But perhaps you're right. Let's head for the beach. A swim in the ocean is just what you need to wash off the grime of traveling."

Alex showed Cassie to her room, then left her to

unpack. Cassie spent the first few minutes staring at her surroundings. She actually had a canopy bed, with a bedspread patterned in bright reds and blues. There were baskets everywhere, plus beige wicker tables and chairs. A charming wooden carousel horse stood in front of the big bay window. A blue bandanna was tied around his neck, as if some child had once used it for a rein.

For a long moment, Cassie perched in the window seat. Gazing out the window, she could just make out a patch of white sandy beach and gently rolling waves.

"Ready?" Alex stuck her head in the door. She was wearing a bright cover-up over her swimsuit. "I told Fidelia, Aunt Owena's housekeeper, that we'll be having tea in the green room."

"Oh, Alex, this so lovely, I could stay here for months."

"I'll talk to Aunt Owena and see what can be arranged," Alex said with a smile. "Right now I'm dying for some scones and a cup of tea. I'll meet you downstairs."

Suddenly Cassie was hungry, too. Slipping out of her wrinkled traveling clothes, she tugged on a suit, grabbed a cover-up, and ran back downstairs.

Alex sat leisurely over her two cups of Earl Grey tea and scones. Sipping her tea, Cassie tried to act the proper British lady, but she could barely wait to get outside.

On their way to the beach, the girls passed the boat where they had left Keir.

"Would you like to join us?" Alex called out.

For a moment Keir seemed to hesitate. "Go on, I'll catch up," he called back.

"I'll race you," Alex said to Cassie, kicking off her sandals. She ran down the packed sand near the ocean's edge.

Cassie sprinted after her through the waves, sending wading birds into tiny explosions of flight.

They ran until they reached the spot that Alex had said was called Treasure Beach. The small cove, formed by a long spit of land that branched off the island, sparkled with clear, calm water.

Laughing, they threw off their robes and plunged into the warm water. Ten minutes later they were floating on the gentle waves when Keir dived into the surf and sent sheets of water into their faces.

"Keir!" screamed Alex, splashing him back. "Act your age."

"I am," he shouted, laughing. "Today I feel twelve."

Cassie looked on at Alex's and Keir's water battle. She wondered about Keir. Was he always so good-natured and playful?

"Well, what do you think?" Keir asked, swimming up beside Cassie.

"About what?" Cassie stopped swimming and treaded water.

"About Florida, of course. Aren't you a city girl? Is this your first trip to the ocean?" He was getting in all the questions.

"I think I'll stay a while. Ouch!" Cassie jumped and pulled up her foot. "Something bit me."

"Probably one of our pet sharks," Keir teased, his eyes laughing at her.

"I know you're kidding me. But what kinds of sea creatures actually live here?" Cassie couldn't help but look around. The water wasn't that clear.

"Well, crocodiles and—"

"Okay, okay. I may be a city girl," said Cassie, "but I know there aren't any crocodiles in the ocean."

"Arghh, help!" Swimming away from Cassie, Keir suddenly began to flail his arms and call out. His head went under twice, then stayed there.

"Keir?" said Cassie, twirling around in the water. "Where are you? You're teasing me, aren't you? Keir!" Cassie turned and waved at Alex. "Alex, come here."

Alex swam toward her. "Where is he? Where's Keir?"

Both girls treaded water, looking all around them. Cassie was sure Keir was going to erupt from the water at any second. But there was no sign of him. A minute passed. The only sounds were the slosh of waves and the screech of a seagull overhead.

"He's gone," whispered Cassie. A shiver of fear ran the full length of her spine.

After several minutes went by, Cassie and Alex were as puzzled as they were frightened. They got out of the water and stood on the beach. They peered out into the cove, but there was no sign of Keir.

"He's too good a swimmer to drown," said Alex.

"Are there any sharks in the cove?" asked Cassie.

Alex shuddered. "I don't think so." She shaded her eyes and scanned the horizon again. "I suppose he could have climbed out onto that spit of land, but with the tide so high, it's almost underwater."

The small mangrove-tangled stretch of sand was just visible. "We'd have spotted him," said Cassie.

"Has anyone here seen my twin brother, Keir?" said a low voice behind them.

"Keir! How could you?" said Alex, whirling around.

"We thought you were dead." Cassie put her hands on her hips and scowled at the unrepentant young man. He grinned back at her, obviously pleased with his trick.

"Don't ever do that again," said Alex.

"I want to know how you disappeared like that," said Cassie, her curiosity aroused. "You must be able to hold your breath for several minutes."

"I'm part fish," confessed Keir. "Anyone raised down here is. Didn't anybody tell you that?"

"I'm afraid they didn't," answered Alex. She marched down the beach toward Owena's house. Cassie could tell she was still a bit irritated by Keir's trick.

Keir gave Cassie an ironic salute and dove back into the water for another swim. Smiling now at the way Keir had fooled them, Cassie followed Alex back to the house.

"It's time I introduced you to Keir's mother," said Alex when they had reached Owena's. "Fidelia's usually in the kitchen. She can tell us what time Owena has planned dinner."

The sunny yellow kitchen had rustic wooden cupboards lining the walls. Copper-bottomed pans hung around the island in the center, which held a chopping block, burners, and two ovens. In a bay window garden, fragrant herbs grew in a dozen small clay pots.

"Fidelia, I'd like you to meet my guest, Cassandra Best, from Ohio," Alex said to the black-haired woman standing at the stove. "She'll be sleeping in the red room."

Fidelia was wearing a yellow flower-print dress, characteristic of her native Jamaica. Though her dress matched the cheery yellow kitchen, the woman who turned to look at Cassie was in anything but a sunny mood. Scowling, she gave Cassie a quick glance and turned back to the stove. Her eyes were the same dark brown as Keir's, but not nearly as friendly.

"Nice to meet you," said Cassie, taken aback at the cold reception.

Fidelia gave Cassie only a curt nod in return.

"What time is dinner?" asked Alex.

"Eight o'clock," murmured the housekeeper.

Alex gave Cassie a sign, and they turned and left the kitchen.

"What was that all about?" asked Cassie, as they headed for the stairs.

"I'm sorry, Cassie," said Alex. "Fidelia's been moody ever since I arrived."

Moody was a polite way of putting it, thought Cassie. She'd never felt so unwelcome in her life.

"Cassandra, I've been looking forward to meeting you all day," called a friendly voice. From the direc-

25

tion of the green room came a woman who was obviously Owena Madison.

"Pleased to meet you, Mrs. Madison," said Cassie. "I'm afraid you caught us looking a mess." Cassie was suddenly conscious of her wet bathing suit, matted hair, and sandy thongs.

"Oh, we're very informal here. It comes from living on the beach." Owena's face lit up with a warm, if somewhat forced smile. "Please call me Owena."

Owena put out a slender hand and took Cassie's. Tall and aristocratic-looking, Owena wore a long, cream-colored dress of homespun cotton. Around her shoulders rested a woven blue-and-orange shawl. Her silver hair was swept into a French twist.

"Hurry and clean up, then join us in the dining room. We have so much to talk about." Despite her gracious manner, Owena seemed a bit tense as she walked away.

Cassie had showered and was looking over her few clothes when Alex burst into the room.

"Are you ready, Cassie?" asked Alex. She had put on a long skirt and a brightly embroidered blouse. On her feet were ornate sandals.

Cassie had planned to wear a simple lavender skirt and a short-sleeved silk shirt. She took one look at Alex and said with dismay, "Oh! I should have realized you dress for dinner here."

Alex laughed. "I keep forgetting how casual you

Americans are. Come on. I have plenty of long skirts, even one that will match that top." She dashed out of the room and returned a moment later with a richly patterned silk skirt.

"Alex, that's beautiful! I'd love to wear it." Cassie changed and the two girls went down to dinner together.

It had gotten dark while she and Alex were dressing. The glassed-in dining room was lit by tin lanterns in the corners of the room. A softly lit chandelier hung from the center of the ceiling. The long, antique dining table was set for five.

Owena and her companions stood up when Cassie and Alex entered the room. "Cassandra, I'd like you to meet Whitford Bromfield," she said. The man who took Cassie's hand was handsome, with intense blue-gray eyes and thick white hair. "He's my nearest neighbor."

"Pleased to meet you, Cassandra," said Whit. "This is my granddaughter, Fran, who's visiting me for the summer. Fran, you and Cassandra should have a lot in common. Alex told me that Cassandra's studying to be an actress. Fran was in all her high school plays," Whit explained to Cassie as they took their places at the table.

Fran Bromfield was a short, stocky girl with a heart-shaped face and curly blond hair. Her green eyes looked defiant as she said to Cassie, "Acting seems childish to me now. I've found better things to do with my time."

"Oh, really," said Cassie politely, ignoring the young woman's rudeness.

"Yes, I'm studying marine biology at the University," Fran answered. "I'm going to be a scientist."

"Since she's so serious about life all of a sudden, I've put her to work this summer," Whit said, looking at his granddaughter fondly. "She's one of my best divers."

Cassie looked at Fran closely and wondered how much she knew about Whit's troubled expedition.

Fran started to eat the shrimp appetizer that Fidelia had served while they talked.

Whit seemed eager to talk about Sand Dollar Key. "Did Alex tell you how isolated our island is?" he asked Cassie. "People have tried to get us to sell pieces of it, but we prefer to keep it to ourselves." He looked at Owena and smiled. Cassie could see there was a warm, longtime friendship between the two.

"I'll bet it was even more isolated when you moved here, Aunt Owena," said Alex. "Weren't you scared?"

"I'll admit I was nervous at first, but I came to love it. We didn't even have electricity when Jim and I came here." Aunt Owena ladled soup from the tureen Fidelia had placed before her. "Now, as you see, I still prefer the soft light of the lanterns."

28

Fidelia bent over Cassie, replacing the appetizer plate with a bowl of steaming soup. Without looking at her, Cassie could feel Fidelia's hostility. Alex had said Fidelia was moody. Rude was more like it. There must be a reason for this behavior.

"Were you and your husband here alone?" Cassie asked Owena, trying to shrug off her uncomfortable feeling.

"Yes, in the beginning," answered Owena. "But soon Fidelia and her husband arrived from Jamaica. Fidelia became my good friend. I don't know what I'd do without her." Owena smiled at her housekeeper. Cassie wondered what kind of company anyone as hostile as Fidelia could be for Owena.

"What did your husband do?" asked Cassie. "Was he a treasure hunter?"

"Gracious, no." Owena laughed softly. "Jim was a businessman, but he was fascinated by sunken treasure. He became a collector and amateur archaeologist. Whit is the treasure hunter, the sole owner of his business, *Tesoros Hallados*."

"That means treasure discovered," Alex chimed in. "Whit's life is so romantic. I'm going to interview Whit for my article as soon as he finds the ship he's looking for," Alex went on. "He's promised to find it while I'm here."

"Maybe I'd better lay one myth to rest," said Whit. He made a wry face. "After twenty years, there's not much romance left. I am deeply in debt,

29

and I wonder every day if I can hang on any longer. I wish I had as much faith in finding that ship as you do, Alex.''

''But you find things all the time, don't you?'' asked Cassie, handing her empty soup bowl to Fidelia, who cleared the second course. As interesting as the conversation was, Cassie was growing a little impatient. She wondered if everyone was avoiding the discussion of Whit's problems because Fran was present. ''You must get excited about your finds, Whit, or you'd quit.''

''Let me put it this way, Cassandra. I've lowered myself halfway into a very deep well. I can't afford to go much deeper, and I can't afford to haul myself out.''

''Or you *won't*,'' said Owena accusingly. ''Don't let him fool you, Cassandra. He's obsessed by treasure-hunting and always will be. Gold fever, they call it here. Once you catch it, you don't get over it easily.''

Conversation continued while Fidelia served the rest of the meal, though her scowling face seemed to cast a pall over everyone's spirits. As the housekeeper left the room, Fran remarked, ''I see Fidelia's her usual charming self tonight.'' Fran got up from the table. ''Fidelia was never very cheerful, but lately she's become positively funereal.'' With that, Fran left the dining room.

Owena turned to Cassie. ''Alex probably told you

about the diver who disappeared in the storm a month ago, Cassandra. He was Fidelia's older son, Keir's brother. Fidelia hasn't been herself since."

"How did it happen?" Cassie asked Whit, glad she could speak more openly.

"Storms come up quickly down here." Whit lay down his fork and brushed his mouth with his napkin. "We were all diving from the *Whitewater*. Before we could get all the divers back onto the boat, the seas got extremely rough. One of my men said he saw Paolo struggling to get back. He was a very strong swimmer. And, of course, we tried to reach him, but the waves were so high, I thought we were going to capsize. Before we could get to him, he disappeared beneath the waves. We stayed in the area all night and searched the next morning. Nothing."

Cassie could see that Whit was still blaming himself for the loss of one of his crew. But she was sure he had done all he could to find Paolo. She knew what dangerous work treasure-hunting could be.

"Whit and I were discussing his newest problems before you got here," said Owena, pouring coffee. "He's on the verge of discovery, but someone seems determined to stop him. More and more things keep going wrong. He's convinced someone is vandalizing his operation."

"Deliberately keeping you from finding the treasure?" asked Cassie.

"This is no secret," said Whit, lowering his voice

anyhow. "But I know I'm just this far from finding that ship." He raised his hand and spread two fingers an inch apart. "My crew is certain, too. We're all working day and night. It's the ship I've been searching for all these years—the *Madreperla*."

"*Madreperla*," repeated Cassie. "Mother-of-pearl," she translated, calling on her two years of high school Spanish.

"Right," said Whit. "But the ship contains much more than pearls. Whoever finds the *Madreperla* will have a fortune to rival that of the *Atocha*."

"One of the richest discoveries in the Keys," Cassie mused aloud, getting more and more excited. A bit of gold fever was gaining hold of her imagination. "Go on, please. I didn't mean to interrupt your story. What's on the *Madreperla*?"

"Since you know about the *Atocha*, you also know that its treasure yielded over four hundred million dollars. We think the *Madreperla* was carrying almost as many gold and silver bars and probably more in jewelry, antiquities, and emeralds from the mines of Colombia. There was nearly always more treasure on the ships than was registered on the cargo lists. People lied about how much they were carrying because they didn't want to pay duty to the king of Spain. Many smuggled personal riches on board." Whit's voice rose with his enthusiasm. Cassie could tell how desperately he wanted to find that treasure.

"We're all excited about the money, of course,"

Owena joined in the conversation. "But tell them what else you think is on the ship, Whit."

"One of the finest archaeological artifacts ever found on a shipwreck," Whit said proudly. "The *Madreperla* carried a golden statue of a jaguar that had been sculpted for the queen of Spain."

"And it had a collar studded with emeralds, and two huge emeralds set as its eyes," added Owena.

"How do we know so much about the sculpture?" asked Alex.

"The colonial government was sending the jaguar to the queen of Spain as a gesture of respect and allegiance to the crown," answered Whit. "They sent a letter to her describing the statue. They even included a sketch."

Cassie felt it was time she began her investigation. "Do you think someone has let you hunt for this treasure, so that he can take it away now that you're close to finding it?"

"Technically I have the salvage rights from the state of Florida," said Whit. "But not everyone follows the rules."

"What is supposed to happen when you find the treasure?" asked Cassie.

"After it's been carefully examined by an archaeologist, I turn it over to the state. They return seventy-five percent of it to me."

"But seventy-five percent of four hundred million dollars—" started Cassie.

"Isn't chicken feed," finished Whit. "I'll be able to pay back the foundation—they've invested way too much in my operation. Then I can pay off my other investors, and have enough left over for my old age. If I can hang on, that is." The energy went out of Whit's voice.

"Most treasure hunters don't have the chance to get old," muttered Fidelia, returning to clear the coffee cups.

Her unexpected comment startled everyone in the room. The silence continued until Fidelia had finished and left the room again.

"Whit's costs have doubled with the repairs he's had to make," Owena said, finishing his story. "He's even had to buy new equipment."

"Are you sure the setbacks aren't just accidents?" asked Cassie.

"Absolutely," answered Whit. "First we found sand clogging the engine of the *Whitewater*. That couldn't happen by accident. Overhauling it cost me a lot of time and money. Then my older boat, the *Sea Adventurer*, disappeared one night."

"Was it stolen?" asked Cassie.

"Stolen and probably sunk," said Whit grimly. "We looked everywhere but couldn't find it—even though it's almost impossible to hide a boat.

"And finally, bolts were loosened on the winch we use to pull up heavy salvage. The winch fell on one of my men and broke his leg."

"Could the bolts have loosened over time without anyone noticing?" asked Cassie.

"We check every bolt and screw each time the winch is used. My equipment is old and sometimes held together with bailing wire, but I'm adamant about safety. We're too much at risk in this business as it is." Whit shook his head. "No, it was deliberate."

"When did this vandalism start, Whit?" asked Cassie. Suddenly a thought occurred to her. "Did you have any problems before Paolo disappeared?"

"Come to think of it, I didn't." Whit frowned. "What are you getting at, Cassandra?"

"I'm not sure yet," Cassie answered honestly. "Do you have any enemies?" It was an obvious question, but Cassie felt she had to ask it.

"Everyone has people who are envious of what they're doing," Whit replied. "And there's a lot of rivalry among treasure hunters here. But enemies, no."

"Alex mentioned that you don't want to call the police in," said Cassie.

"That's right," said Whit. "I don't have enough evidence to have anyone arrested. In fact, I have little evidence at all."

"I hope you can help us, Cassandra," said Owena.

"I don't mean to offend anyone, Owena," said Whit. He looked grim. "But I find it hard to believe that this lovely young lady will discover anything that I haven't found already. But I welcome all the help I can get, Cassandra. Do you want to get started tomorrow?''

"Of course," said Cassie, smiling.

At that moment Fidelia appeared in the doorway. Her face looked even more disapproving than usual. "Mr. Bromfield, someone is here to see you," she announced.

A young man pushed past Fidelia and into the dining room. "I'm sorry to disrupt your dinner, Whit. But you'd better come down to the marina right away," he said.

"What's the matter, Tom?" asked Whit, rising from his chair.

"It's the *Anhinga*, sir. Somebody's smashed your new sonar equipment. Badly."

Whit's face turned red with anger and he pounded his fist on the table. "I'm so close to finding that treasure! Who could be trying to stop me?"

Cassie shivered. Someone must be getting pretty desperate to vandalize Whit's boats so often.

"The *Anhinga*'s your new boat, isn't it, Whit?" Owena asked. She looked dazed.

"That sonar equipment was supposed to give me the last push I need," said Whit. He strode to the door. "I'm going down to the marina. Come on, Tom." The two men left the house.

"Can we go, too, Aunt Owena?" asked Alex.

"I think we've all done enough for one day," Owena answered, her face drained. "I'm sure Cassandra is exhausted from her trip. Why don't we get some rest.''

Cassie knew she'd have trouble getting to sleep after this latest development, but she followed Owena's suggestion. Surprisingly, she slept soundly.

In the morning, eager to get on with the investigation, Cassie got dressed quickly and went downstairs.

She was just in time to hear Fidelia talking to Owena in the kitchen.

''Mr. Bromfield's jinxed, I tell you. Jinxed,'' said the housekeeper. ''If he knows what's good for him, he'll stop this treasure nonsense. He should leave all that old stuff on the bottom of the ocean where it belongs.''

Owena sighed as if she'd had this argument many times before. ''It's not old stuff, Fidelia. It's gold and silver and jewels worth millions. And its historical value is limitless. Whit says he's on the verge of finding it, and I believe him.''

''He's a fool,'' said Fidelia. ''You're all fools. People keep getting hurt, and you ignore all the warnings.'' Carrying a tray of juice and rolls, she brushed past Cassie, who was coming in the doorway.

''Have you heard from Whit, Owena?'' asked Cassie.

''Not yet,'' Owena answered. ''I doubt that he's had time to call me.'' She was arranging some fruit on a platter. ''Cassandra, you seem quite young to be investigating crimes. Diving for treasure is a dangerous business to begin with, and it's not without its pirates. People become pretty ruthless when a million dollars is at stake."

"My age is an advantage, Owena," Cassie said. "No one expects me to be watching them."

"Well, promise me you'll be careful." Owena picked up the platter and started into the dining room.

"I will be. I don't even need to promise."

"No matter how careful you are, you're headed for deep trouble, girl." Fidelia's voice resonated behind her and almost made Cassie jump. "Stop meddling with something you don't understand. Go away and don't come back."

Fidelia sounded so serious that Cassie almost felt like laughing. But she didn't want to make an enemy of the superstitious housekeeper. Instead, she ignored her and went to meet Alex in the dining room.

After Owena had poured coffee for Cassie and tea for Alex, she said in a soft voice, "Please make allowances for Fidelia, Cassandra. I heard her warn you. She wasn't always so negative, but her son's death has made her hate anything having to do with treasure-hunting."

Cassie nodded sympathetically. It must be awful to be so full of bitterness, she thought.

While they ate breakfast, the girls made plans to

go into Key West. Owena would go with them and shop for supplies. Alex would start doing background work for her article, and Cassie would start her investigation.

An unusually quiet Keir dropped them all off at the marina. Owena pointed out Whit's office, which was housed in a retired boat called the *Riptide*. Then she left them and went on her way.

When Alex and Cassie had climbed aboard, Whit came over to greet them. "This is the last straw," he said at once. "The equipment has been totally smashed. I can't tell how long it will take to repair."

Cassie was eager to get to work. "Can I see the *Anhinga?*" she asked.

"I'll take you over in a moment," Whit answered. "I've got some work to do here first."

"Then can I look at your records for the last couple of years?" asked Cassie.

"Sure, if you think that will help," said Whit. "I don't have any secrets from anyone. Everyone knows I'm on the verge of finding the *Madreperla*. But everyone also knows I'm on the edge as far as finances go."

"It sounds as if someone is trying to push you over the edge," commented Cassie. She began to flip through the big record book that Whit handed to her. She could see at once that there was much more money going out of the organization than coming in.

She looked over page after page while Whit made several phone calls. It didn't take Cassie long to discover where Whit's money went. When he salvaged anything from the ocean, he sold it and shared the profit with the company's investors. His share went right back into his equipment.

"How many boats do you have, Whit?" asked Cassie, between his calls.

"Right now, four," Whit replied. "But three are just barely safe. That's why I invested in the *Anhinga*. We have six sites that we're working on. I found cannons from the *Madreperla* on one of them, and then a few gold bars—enough to get my permit. The main treasure—the mother lode—is still eluding us."

"Why didn't the Spanish try to salvage their own wrecks?" asked Alex. "Especially if they were worth so much?"

"They did, but their equipment was primitive," Whit said. "A diver could stay underwater for only as long as he could hold his breath. Modern treasure-hunting didn't become possible until 1943. All those wrecks just lay there waiting for four hundred years."

"What happened in 1943?" asked Alex.

"Jacques Cousteau invented the self-contained underwater breathing apparatus," Whit explained.

"Scuba." Cassie looked up from the record book.

"Yes. Scuba gear suddenly made shallow-water diving a new sport. And treasure hunters recognized the possibilities, too." Whit got up from his chair, looking suddenly restless. "Come on, girls, let me show you where the *Anhinga* is."

Whit led them out of his floating office and down the dock to his new boat. From the dock, Cassie could see that the *Anhinga* was much more modern and up-to-date than the *Riptide*. The more she saw of Whit's operation, the more impressed she was by its size and scope.

"You must work with a lot of divers," she said. "Have you hired anyone new recently?"

"Divers come and go quickly," Whit answered. "The romance disappears after twelve to sixteen hours a day in the water seven days a week—on about two dollars an hour pay."

"Who'd work for that?" Alex asked.

"Divers are mostly young guys looking for adventure, not big paychecks." Whit laughed. "And to tell you the truth, no one has gotten a paycheck recently."

"Don't you get any women divers?" asked Cassie.

"Very few," said Whit. "My wife dived. She was one of the best. And Fran learned to dive here when she was just a little girl. Owena's a fine diver, too."

Whit called out to a man coming toward them on

the dock. "Todd, there's someone here I'd like you to meet."

A short, well-built young man strolled over. Though Cassie guessed he was in his late twenties, she sensed immediately that he had the confidence of someone much older. His hair was bleached almost white from the sun.

"Alex and Cassandra, this is Todd Wrightson, our resident archaeologist," said Whit. Turning to Todd, he went on, "Alex is Owena's niece, Todd. She's here from England to write about the foundation's party. Cassandra is her friend. She came along to play tourist."

"Are you from England, too?" Todd asked Cassie, fingering the gold coin around his neck.

Cassie saw that Whit wore a gold doubloon, too. Doubloons must be standard dress for treasure hunters, she thought.

"No, I'm from Ohio," said Cassie, smiling. "What kind of archaeology are you trained in?"

"Marine. I have degrees from several schools. The last in California." Todd seemed proud of his accomplishments.

"Todd came to me about as highly recommended as a scientist can be," said Whit. "He's recently made some interesting discoveries off the Great Barrier Reef."

"Australia," Cassie said, impressed. "Do you

think Whit's as close to finding the *Madreperla* as he thinks he is?''

''We'll find it any day now.'' Todd spoke with an air of absolute authority. ''When we do, I'll bring up the jaguar myself. Finding that piece will make us all famous.''

''Your future will be secure, so to speak?'' Cassie asked. It was hard to resist teasing him, he took himself so seriously.

''My future has never been in doubt,'' Todd said. Though he spoke with a self-esteem bordering on conceit, he tried to soften the remark with a smile. ''With the jaguar to my credit, however, I can write my own ticket.''

Todd's as obsessed about his job as Whit is, thought Cassie. And he regards finding the jaguar as a personal challenge.

''If you don't need me for an hour or so, Whit, I have business in town,'' said Todd.

''Go ahead, Todd,'' said Whit. The archaeologist gave Cassie and Alex a somewhat stiff smile and headed back up the dock.

The girls followed Whit onto the deck of the *Anhinga* and into the cabin. The mess left by last night's intruder was sickening. It looked as if someone had taken a sledgehammer to the sonar equipment.

Tom, the man who'd reported the damage to Whit, was in the cabin. Another man, his head partly bandaged, stood beside him. Whit introduced him as Larry. He'd been on guard the night before and had been knocked out by the intruder.

"Did you get a look at your assailant?" asked Cassie.

"No," answered Larry. "It was a dark night, not a star to be seen. I was up on deck having a smoke when I felt a tremendous blow to my head. I saw stars then." He smiled humorlessly. "The next thing I knew, I was waking up in an ambulance."

"Have you found any clues at all?" asked Cassie.

"Only this." Tom held up a gold chain, the clasp broken. On it dangled half a gold doubloon. "I found it in the cabin doorway this morning."

"I know that chain," said Cassie slowly. "It's Keir's. He was wearing it yesterday. But what could it be doing here?"

"Do you know my head diver?" asked Whit.

As if on cue, Keir himself appeared in the doorway.

"Keir is your head diver?" asked Cassie.

"You thought I was a beach bum, didn't you," said Keir, giving her his familiar teasing smile. Then he turned to Whit. "I thought I heard my name. What's up?"

"Is this yours?" asked Whit, holding out the chain and its ornament.

"Where'd you find that?" Keir grabbed at the doubloon. "Paolo gave this to me years ago. I thought I'd lost it forever." He fumbled with the clasp.

"We found it on the *Anhinga* this morning," Whit said slowly. "After the break-in. What was it doing here?"

"I don't know." Keir looked confused, then defensive. "Whit, you can't believe I wrecked your new boat. Why, I'd have no reason—" He broke off abruptly.

"What are we supposed to think, Keir?" asked Tom.

"How dare you accuse me!" Keir said, his voice rising. He was working himself into a rage. "You take back your insinuations or else!" He breathed heavily, his fists slowly clenching and unclenching.

"I will not!" Tom shouted back. "Ever since your brother . . ."

Tom never got a chance to finish his sentence. Keir's fist shot out and landed on his jaw. With a low moan, Tom went down and collapsed at Cassie's feet.

Chapter 5

*I*n a flash, Whit strode over and restrained Keir. "Get a hold of yourself," he said, roughly shaking the young man. "No one is accusing you of anything."

Keir took a deep breath. Already the anger seemed to be seeping out of him. "I'm okay, Whit. You can let me go now. I don't know what comes over me sometimes."

"Learn to restrain yourself," said Whit curtly. He released Keir's arms and went over to where Cassie and Alex were bending over the unconscious Tom.

"He's coming to," said Cassie. "The blow only grazed him." Tom moaned slightly, then sat up holding his jaw.

"Let's get him out into the fresh air," said Whit. "Give me a hand, Larry." The two men helped Tom to his feet. With a hand under each of Tom's arms, they eased him out of the cabin.

"I'm sorry about that," said Keir to Cassie and Alex. His voice still sounded shaky. "Sometimes I let my temper run away with me."

You certainly do, thought Cassie. Aloud, she said, "Do you know when you lost the doubloon? You were wearing it yesterday when you were swimming with us."

"I don't know." Keir looked away, as if he were trying to evade the question. "I just noticed it was gone this morning." He seemed weary. "Look, I didn't have anything to do with damaging Whit's equipment. I just wish someone would believe me."

He looked straight at Cassie as he spoke. Then he added abruptly, "I'll see you around," and left.

Cassie wasn't sure what to think. Beneath his surface good humor, Keir was a very angry young man. But what was he angry about? And was he so angry that he would sabotage Whit's operation?

Cassie and Alex returned to the deck. "I've got to get back to work," Whit said, coming up to them. "You two can find something to do, I'm sure. Do either of you dive?"

"I do," said Alex. "Every time my father goes to Australia or the Caribbean, I go along. I've been diving since I was twelve."

"I didn't know that," said Cassie, looking at Alex

with admiration. "There's not much deep-sea diving in Ohio. I have to admit I've never tried it. I'd like to learn, though. And learning how to dive might help me in my investigation."

"Maybe," said Whit dubiously. He turned around. "Fran, come over here. I have an extra job for you."

His granddaughter excused herself from the conversation she was having and walked toward them. Like the rest of the crew, she was wearing a bathing suit and cut-offs. Everyone seemed ready to go into the water at a moment's notice.

"Cassandra could use some diving instruction, Fran. Take care of it, will you? Thanks." Whit patted his granddaughter on the shoulder and excused himself. Whit must be under a lot of pressure, Cassie thought. He's not usually so brusque.

"Do you have your suits?" Fran asked Cassie and Alex when Whit had left. She seemed resigned to her job.

"Sure do," said Cassie. Alex and Cassie carried small duffels and had packed bathing suits along with their cameras and writing materials.

"I'll start you in the pool in town, Cassie," said Fran. "I'll need to check you out, too, Alex, before you can dive in these waters."

They went to the city pool. Fortunately, Cassie was a good swimmer and had even earned her senior life-saving certificate at the local Milltown

YMCA. She surprised herself by taking to scuba diving immediately. It was remarkably easy once she had learned to breathe slowly and evenly through her mouthpiece.

By late morning, Fran was ready to supervise the girls in a shallow stretch of ocean. Back at the marina, she borrowed the small runabout that was tied to Whit's floating office and took them to a nearby cove.

"You'll be fine," she said, when Cassie and Alex had come back on shore after a successful dive. "If you can swim, you can dive." A licensed instructor, Fran could even award them certificates that proved they'd passed all the tests.

"I doubt that's true for everyone," said Alex, "but I'm proud of you, Cassie." She circled her friend's waist with her arm and hugged her. "Now we can have some fun."

"Could we have some lunch first?' asked Cassie. "All this exercise has made me ravenous."

"Good idea," agreed Alex. "Would you like to join us, Fran?" The girl had become more friendly in the course of the morning.

"I can't," Fran answered, a little too quickly. "I have plans. Make sure you're back at the marina at about three, though. I'll see if we can take one of the boats out for a real dive."

"Right-o!" said Alex. "I'm dying to see the reef. I understand it's beautiful."

During lunch at a coffee shop near the marina, Cassie asked, "Do you think I'm ready for my first dive?"

"You won't know until you try," Alex pointed out. "I think you'll love diving, Cassie."

As they ate their hamburgers, Cassie turned the conversation to the subject of vandalism.

"I don't want to believe Keir caused all that damage to Whit's boat," Cassie said, "but I'm not sure he's telling us the truth. It seems that he must have been on board sometime last night."

"Couldn't someone else have left his necklace to make it look as if Keir had been there?" asked Alex. "To set him up?"

"Certainly," said Cassie. "But he would have had to get the doubloon away from Keir first. How easy do you think that would be? No, there's something that Keir's not telling us." They finished their lunch in silence, each mulling over the mystery of Keir's behavior.

When they stepped on board the *Whitewater* a short time later, they discovered that Whit was sending his boats out to work the dive sites. He had decided that, ruined equipment or not, he couldn't afford to waste another day.

"Is our equipment on board?" Cassie asked Fran, who had promised to help them on their dive.

"Probably, but it doesn't matter," Fran answered. "There's a pile of tanks and hoses here. We always have extras."

Both Todd and Keir were on board. Keir came over to talk to them immediately. He seemed surprisingly cheerful. Was he always subject to such violent mood swings? Cassie wondered.

"How's Tom?" she asked, opening the conversation.

Keir looked chagrined. "He's much better now," he said. "We've had a talk, and everything's okay."

Todd came over to join them. "So you're making your first dive?" he asked. "You must be nervous."

"Excited, not nervous," Cassie corrected him. "Fran's a good teacher." Cassie looked at Todd's equipment. It looked different from Keir's. "Do you always carry two tanks, Todd?"

Todd's face flushed despite his tan. Before he could answer, Keir said, "Todd's a real sissy, Cassandra. He has this fear of running out of air, so he carries an extra tank."

Cassie looked at Todd to see if Keir were teasing.

The older man didn't seem to take offense at Keir's remarks. "I'm claustrophobic," he said, grinning sheepishly. "It's a terrible problem for a marine archaeologist, isn't it? When I first started diving, I wasn't sure I could do it. In addition to being uncomfortable underwater, I had this morbid fear of running out of air. I would choke just thinking about it."

"You must have worked really hard to overcome it," said Alex, admiration in her voice.

"When I've made up my mind, I can do anything," Todd said, somewhat pompously. "One of my instructors suggested the extra tank. That helps a lot. Most of the time I don't even think about the phobia anymore—that is, until someone like this fish reminds me." Todd gave Keir an odd look. "Keir and Paolo used to show off by diving without tanks at all. Totally impractical."

"We used to compete to see who could hold his breath the longest," Keir said. "Once, because I had to surface first, Paolo got a gold piece that should have been mine." Keir fingered the doubloon on the repaired chain around his neck.

"So he shared it with you?" asked Cassie. Now she knew why the doubloon meant so much to Keir.

"Yeah, he cut it in half. He always wore the other half." Keir got up and walked quickly to the other side of the ship.

Todd stared at Keir's back as he left. "He'll never get over Paolo's death," Todd said. "I think he blames Whit, but he keeps his feelings to himself."

"What happened to Paolo that night, Todd?" asked Cassie. She wanted to hear the story from someone other than Whit.

By and large, Todd's account of the storm agreed with Whit's. But then he added, "I don't blame Whit in any way for losing Paolo, but he should have left the site and come in long before that storm hit."

"He told us the storm came up quickly," Alex said, defending her aunt's friend.

"Any sailor who's been down here as long as Whit has can read the weather," said Todd. "I think Whit planned to ride out the storm and go back to work. But the winds were worse than he expected."

Was Whit actually negligent? Cassie wondered. Or was Todd judging his actions too harshly?

More important, did Keir think Whit was responsible for his brother's death? If so, that could account for Keir's anger.

Fran came up and took her mind off the problem. "Here's gear for you both," she said. As she helped Cassie into the harness that held her tank, Fran reviewed the proper procedure.

"First check your air pressure," she reminded the girls. "Then check your regulator. Are you getting plenty of air?" Cassie nodded. "When you get in the water, check your regulator again. And remember to clear your mask if it fogs up."

Cassie slipped into the tank harness, placed her mask on top of her head, and went to stand by the railing. It was a perfect day, with not a cloud in the sky. As their boat sped across the water, she lifted her face to feel the salt air and spray.

A few minutes later, the boat slowed and began circling the dive site. A buoy marked the area that the crew would be investigating. Alex and Fran joined Cassie by the railing. "We'll go down slowly," said Fran. "You follow me."

Cassie tightened the belt that secured the harness holding her air tank. She placed the mouthpiece firmly between her teeth and closed her lips over the rubber. Again she checked to make sure she was getting air and that none was leaking. Everything seemed to be in order.

Signaling to each other, Cassie, Fran, and Alex went down a rope ladder and over the side of the boat into the sparkling blue water.

Immediately Cassie felt she had entered some kind of fairyland. Around her swam fish in every color of the rainbow. They darted in and out of pink and yellow coral reefs that looked like a fantastic playground. Some of the coral branched out like bushes. Others were round and wrinkled, like deserted brains from huge sea creatures.

Fran motioned for them to follow her, but Cassie hardly paid attention. She drifted, kicking her fins only slightly to keep moving. Bubbles from her airhose surrounded her head and rose to the surface. A kind of euphoria settled over her. How wonderful it would be to spend every day exploring this fantastic ocean community, she thought.

Then, without any warning, she stopped getting air. Instinctively, she had started holding her breath. Breathe, Cassie, breathe, she reminded herself. But when she tried, she couldn't get any air. Trying not to panic, she twisted her regulator. Still no air.

She felt as if her lungs would burst. Desperate, she looked around for help. There was no one in sight.

Cassie was alone on the ocean floor. And she knew she couldn't hold her breath long enough to get to the surface.

Don't pass out, Cassie told herself. Your only chance is to surface.

With what little strength she had left, Cassie started swimming toward the circle of light above her. When she felt a hand on her arm, she didn't slow down, but kept moving her arms and legs methodically.

Then someone tugged at her mouthpiece. It was Alex. Her friend had taken the air hose from her own mouth and was offering it to Cassie. It took Cassie several seconds to start breathing normally. Then she gave the mouthpiece back to Alex.

Slowly they surfaced, "buddy" breathing.

"*Ahhgh*," Cassie gasped when her head popped out of the ocean. She drew in deep breaths of sweet, clean air. It was a full minute before she had recovered enough to talk to Alex.

"What happened?" Alex asked.

"I don't know," Cassie said, still clutching Alex's arm for support. "Suddenly I was out of air. I didn't realize it until I was desperate. I was holding my breath without thinking."

"Did you check everything before you went down?" Alex asked.

"Of course I did. That was one of the first things Fran taught us. I thought I had plenty of air."

Alex looked at the gauge on Cassie's tank. "Well, this registers empty. Maybe it has a leak. You certainly didn't use up all that air in the few minutes we were underwater."

Cassie looked at the pressure valve. "Look, Alex, it's open slightly."

"Then it would have been leaking air for some time," said Alex. "There would have been a lot of bubbles."

"There were, but I didn't know that wasn't normal," said Cassie.

At that moment Fran popped to the surface. "Hey, what's wrong?" she asked. "I finally realized neither of you was behind me." Fran looked at Cassie and knew she'd had trouble. "Cassandra, what happened?"

"I ran out of air."

Fran looked upset. "Did you check—"

"Yes, I checked the air pressure and the regulator," Cassie said. She started to swim toward the boat. "I'm going back on board."

"I'm not diving without you," declared Alex, starting after Cassie.

"We'll get you another tank and go back down," said Fran. "You need to get over your scare."

"No," Cassie said firmly. "Not now." She needed time to forget her frightening experience. What if she hadn't been so close to the surface? They were diving in fairly shallow water, not nearly the limit for scuba equipment.

Fran climbed out with them and looked around. There were several empty tanks piled on the deck, and a number of full ones. They all looked alike.

"Maybe you picked up the wrong tank," said Fran. "But since you checked your gauge, you knew how much air was in it."

"I didn't check my gauge," said Cassie. "You gave me the tank, remember?"

"That's right, I did." Fran frowned and looked over the pile of gear on the deck. "I could have brought you a partially full tank, Cassandra. But it still would have had enough air for the time we planned to stay down."

Cassie explained about the leaky valve. Fran lifted Cassie's harness off her shoulder and examined the equipment closely. "The regulator might be dirty or worn," she said. "All this gear is old. Whit can't afford anything new. Some of the divers have their own, but not all of them."

Alex had been looking over the other gear on the deck. "Look, an air hose has been cut on this one."

Close inspection revealed that all the equipment piled on deck was damaged in some way.

"This is ridiculous." Fran stood up, hands on her hips. "It's so petty. Why would anyone . . ."

"For the same reason the other things on your grandfather's boats have been vandalized—whatever that reason is," said Cassie.

One by one, other divers from the boat came to the surface, all complaining of some problem with their equipment.

Cassie asked Fran where her equipment had been the night before. "I brought it home with me," Fran answered. "I never leave my equipment lying around. It's very expensive, and I had to save up to buy it." Fran went off to talk to the other divers.

"Where did you get your gear?" Cassie asked Alex. "Yours hasn't been damaged, either."

"This looks like the same equipment I used this morning," Alex pointed out. "And if you remember, Fran got it from the *Anhinga*, not the *Whitewater*."

"It looks as if all the diving equipment that was left on the *Whitewater* last night was damaged," Cassie concluded. "Our vandal must have had a pretty busy night. At first I thought someone must have figured out that I'm a detective." She pulled a towel around her shoulders. "By the way, have you noticed that two people still haven't surfaced?"

"Yes," said Alex. "Obviously there's nothing wrong with Todd's and Keir's equipment, either."

"Where did everyone go?" asked Todd just then, climbing up the boat ladder.

Keir was following him. "Suddenly I realized we were down there alone," he said. "I thought you'd seen a shark."

"Cassie had a bad scare. She ran out of air on the bottom," Alex explained. "Someone vandalized all the gear."

"Except yours," said Cassie to Todd and Keir.

"I never leave my tanks lying around," said Todd. "It's just plain stupid." He held up a severed air hose.

"I take my equipment home at night," Keir said. He crouched beside Cassie. "Are you okay?"

"Yes, now I am. Thanks," she replied.

"Let's go back down," he suggested. "Just for a few minutes."

"Not today, please," Cassie said. "I'd rather wait until tomorrow." She was more tired than she wanted to admit.

Besides, she didn't feel very trusting anymore.

At dinner that night, Owena asked Cassie how the day had gone.

"I did something very careless, I'm afraid," Cassie answered. "I dove down without enough air." She didn't want to alarm Owena. "Actually, I was more embarrassed than frightened once the scare was over. I'm going to try it again tomorrow."

"Oh, Cassandra, I understand how you feel," Owena said. "I've run out of air a couple of times myself. Just forgot to watch the gauge. It's easy to forget time exists down there.

"Why don't you dive off the reef near Sand Dollar Key in the morning?" Owena suggested. "It's an incredibly beautiful place."

Cassie looked at Alex, who nodded. "That would be fine, Owena."

"I'll send Keir to the marina early to get some diving equipment from Whit," said Owena. "Why don't you each keep your equipment here at the house? That way, anytime you want to dive, you'll have it."

And that way, I'll know no one has tampered with it, thought Cassie.

The next morning, Cassie and Alex were down at the dock, piling onto Owena's boat.

"Are you sure we can't persuade you to go, Aunt Owena?" asked Alex. "Whit says you're a good diver."

"I used to be, if I do say so myself. And I loved the reefs," Owena admitted, watching them load the boat. She handed a picnic basket to Keir, who had been persuaded by Owena to take the girls out.

Cassie would just have to trust him.

The noise of the motorboat scared a great blue heron, which flapped its wings and protested with a *squank, squank*. Keir pointed to another bird standing perfectly still on shore. Its long legs looked like two iron rods. On its head it sported one jaunty feather like a headdress. "Bittern," said Keir.

"There seem to be so many types of birds down here," Cassie marveled. Kneeling in the bow of the boat, she absentmindedly trailed her hand in the water.

"Hundreds of them—and fish, too," said Keir. "Including piranha."

Quickly Cassie put her hand in her lap, then felt foolish.

Keir laughed, and Cassie grinned in return. She found it hard to be annoyed with him.

Keir looked off into the distance, lost in thought. Studying him, Cassie realized again how handsome he was. Suddenly his brown eyes sparkled. He looked at Cassie and smiled. She looked away, embarrassed that he'd caught her staring at him.

Just past a shady beach, Keir swung the boat away from the shore. About half a mile out, he stopped the engine.

"This is it?" asked Alex. Keir nodded.

Cassie looked down at the clear water. She

couldn't tell how deep it was. Picking up her air tank, she looked closely at the gauge. It was a full tank. She bent over the side and put the tank in the water. If there were a leak, she'd see bubbles. Slipping on the harness, she carefully took herself through a number of checks. She twisted the regulator, put the mouthpiece between her cheeks, and made sure she was breathing the air from the tank.

Acting is believing, she told herself, recalling her grandmother's old saying. If you act as though you've been diving all your life, you can do it.

Here goes nothing, she said to herself. She sat on the edge of the boat and tumbled over backward into the water. Then she surfaced, cleared her mask, and took several more breaths. A-okay, she signaled to Alex, who was treading water nearby.

"Where's Keir?" Cassie pantomimed, looking at the empty boat.

Alex looked around and shrugged. Then she grabbed Cassie's arm, her face registering shock through the mask. Cassie jerked around to see what she was looking at.

A sea monster was coming straight toward them! Masses of gray-green Spanish moss tumbled around its head like coarse, unruly hair. Crablike claws reached out toward the girls. Alex screamed and kicked away. The mouthpiece fell from Cassie's mouth, but only because she had started to laugh.

"Keir, I know it's you. Leave me alone!" Cassie called. She kicked at him with her flippers.

The "monster" gave a deep laugh. "I'm the Creature from the Black Lagoon," it said in a throaty voice. Then it shook all over, ridding itself of its tangled hair.

"Oh, Keir, when did you put that outfit together?" Alex asked, giggling.

"Tourists very slow this morning," Keir said in a mock Caribbean accent, and grinned.

The trick put Cassie totally at her ease. "Watch out for monsters below," Keir cautioned them as he climbed back onto the boat.

"We will," said Cassie. "Let's go, Alex." She led the way in a surface dive.

Beautifully colored fish—just as exotic as those Cassie had seen on her first dive—swam around and ahead of them. She reached out to touch them, but they kept slightly ahead of her fingers. Sea fans waved in the current that the girls created as they swam by.

Cassie was happy to see Keir swimming after them. He pointed out small creatures that the girls probably would have missed—fish that imitated coral to keep from being eaten; a hermit crab that scurried away at their approach; a small manta ray that shook off some sand and then floated off into the beams of sunlight that sliced through the water from above.

Cassie was startled when an unfamiliar shape

bumped into her. It was a barracuda, its mouth drawn back in a deadly smile. Keir tapped her shoulder and shook his head. He touched the scary fish, then took a scrap of something from his belt and offered it to the toothy jaws. A friendly barracuda? Cassie wondered.

It seemed that only minutes had passed when Keir looked at his watch and motioned them to the surface. Reluctantly Cassie and Alex followed, soon bobbing up beside the boat.

Cassie pushed her mask onto her forehead. "Oh," she said, "I could stay down there forever. Do we have to stop?"

"It's past noon," Keir said, reaching out a hand to help her on board. "Are you still afraid?"

"Not anymore, Keir. Thanks." Cassie knew that Keir had done everything he could to make her second dive better than her first.

"I can't believe we were down there so long," said Alex, slipping off her tank and laying it under a bench on the deck.

"I can. I'm hungry," said Cassie. She stowed her gear and peeked into the picnic basket that Owena had given them.

By the time their boat arrived at the small beach they'd seen earlier, no one had to be persuaded to eat. Cassie munched a ham sandwich and felt wonderful. Perhaps now was the time to talk to Keir, while he was in such a good mood.

"Was that barracuda your pet, Keir?" she asked, to open the conversation.

Keir nodded. "Paolo and I tamed him a long time ago. His name is Boss."

"With those teeth he can be boss anytime I'm around," said Alex, reaching for a pickle.

"Tell me more about Paolo, Keir," said Cassie cautiously. "That is, if you don't mind talking about him."

Keir hesitated, then looked out over the ocean for a moment. "He was an incredible swimmer. He taught me to dive. We spent half our time in the water when we were kids. It's hard for me to believe he drowned, even in a storm."

"Todd said Whit should have called up the divers long before he did," Cassie said. She wanted to put Keir on the spot. "Do you blame him at all for Paolo's death?"

"I try not to think about it," said Keir, his voice tense. He studied his sandwich. "I tell myself that Paolo was at fault, too. He could have come back to the boat earlier. He knew how rough the sea could get." Keir was beginning to get angry.

"When you're diving below the surface, can you tell the ocean is rough on top?" asked Alex.

"Not usually," admitted Keir. "But the storm must have been building long before they went down." His voice began to rise. "That whole crew was responsible for Paolo's death. Sure, divers take

67

chances; it's part of the job. But Whit was a fool to keep the divers out as long as he did. He's obsessed with that treasure." Keir's hands were fists, his knuckles white with tension.

A fool. That's what Fidelia had called Whit, too, Cassie thought.

"What was your mother like before Paolo was drowned, Keir? She seems awfully bitter now," said Cassie.

"She's always been quiet. But we had lots of fun when my dad was alive. We all used to go diving together." Keir paused, remembering. "He was so young when he had his heart attack. Mother could accept his death as inevitable, I guess. But she has never accepted Paolo's. I think she's angry at the world."

"I can see how she might be," Alex said sympathetically.

Much as she liked him, Cassie could tell that Keir was angry at the world, too. But she couldn't tell if he was angry enough to try to keep Whit from finding the treasure he'd been searching for.

Cassie let the conversation drift on to other topics, while they packed up the remains of the picnic and headed back to Owena's beach. By the time they got there, Keir was laughing and joking again. The girls left him and went up to the house to change. Keir was due back at the marina.

"Half an hour?" Alex called to Cassie when they parted in the hall to go to their separate rooms.

"Fine!" Cassie bounced into her room, then came to a dead stop. She let out a screech before she could help herself, then clapped her hand over her mouth.

Over her bed hung a dead chicken. The body was dirty gray, and the head, with its saucy red comb, flopped limply to one side. Around its neck hung a string of ragged red cloth, shells, yellow feathers, and bleached bones.

"It's a voodoo fetish," whispered Cassie.

*A*lex appeared in the doorway, obviously alarmed by Cassie's cry. Owena slipped in behind her.

"Oh, no!" Owena gave a frustrated exclamation, then walked over and released the chicken from its noose. "I'm so sorry, Cassandra. This is obviously a childish prank, and I'll see if I can find out who's behind it."

Cassie already had an idea who could have done such a thing. Only one person in Owena's household came from a part of the world where fetishes were commonplace. But she couldn't accuse anyone without proof.

"Owena," she said hesitantly, "do you think Fidelia could have put the chicken there? I'm sure she overheard us discussing my investigation at dinner. Maybe she thinks I'm just stirring up trouble.''

"I don't know, Cassie." Owena looked distressed. "If I find out this *is* her doing, I'll have to deal with her somehow. But I can't let her go. We've been together too long."

"I'm sure you'll know what to do," said Alex, trying to support her aunt.

Owena stuck her head out the bedroom door and called, "Fidelia, could you please come here for a minute?"

Fidelia appeared so quickly that Cassie knew she must have been just down the hall in her room.

"Do you know anything about this prank, Fidelia?" Owena held up the pathetic-looking chicken.

Fidelia looked frightened. "It means trouble," she said, turning to stare at Cassie. "I've told you before, you're interfering where you're not wanted. This is a warning." Her dark eyes held Cassie's.

"Fidelia, I simply cannot believe that some ghost floated in here and hung that over my bed," Cassie said calmly.

"You'd *better* believe it, young lady," Fidelia said, her voice shaking. "You'll stay away from treasure-hunting if you know what's good for you." Fidelia turned and headed back down the hall.

Owena, Alex, and Cassie looked stunned for a moment. "Girls, what can I say?" said Owena. "I'll have a talk with Fidelia, but I must admit I don't think she's responsible. I hope you can forget this, Cassandra. Now, I'm getting ready to go over to my office in town. Why don't you girls go with me? I think you'll be interested in the foundation's work. And you may gain some information you need there, Cassandra." The girls agreed to go.

Alex stayed with Cassie as they watched Owena carry the chicken out of the room.

"What do you think, Cassie?" asked Alex. "Did Fidelia put the fetish in here to scare you?"

"That's what I thought at first," Cassie answered slowly. "But maybe that's too obvious a solution. Whoever did it knew I'd suspect Fidelia. But did you see how scared she was? I don't think she's that good an actress. She's too superstitious."

"Yes, but if not Fidelia, then who?"

"I suppose anyone with a boat could have come onto the island," Cassie reasoned. "This house is so big, an intruder could have sneaked upstairs even when Owena and Fidelia were here. And they were both away part of the time.

"And then there are the other people who live on the island—Whit, and Fran, and Keir," Cassie added.

"Whit would hardly try to frighten you away from the case," Alex objected. "And arrogant though Fran can be, she warmed up to you considerably yesterday. And Keir? I can't believe he would do anything so mean."

"We must try to be objective, Alex," Cassie told her friend. "I like Keir, too, but he still has the strongest motive for wanting to hurt Whit and frighten me away. If he really hates Whit, his motive may be revenge. We still don't know where he was the night the sonar was smashed."

"But a voodoo fetish, Cassie? When would he have had the time to plant it in your room?"

"Think back to this morning, Alex. He had the time to put together a monster costume while we were with Owena. And he probably knows all about voodoo from his mother.

"No, I'm afraid he stays at the top of my list for now," Cassie concluded.

Owena steered her own boat to Key West. On the way there, she told the girls the history of the Archaeological Foundation they were going to visit.

"My husband was fascinated by what was being found in the wrecks," Owena began. "He didn't want to become involved in Whit's organization, but he believed in what Whit was doing. He thought that if he set up a foundation, most of the treasure could stay here on Key West for people to see."

"How could he collect the treasure without being a treasure hunter himself?" asked Alex.

"Some divers are more interested in money than

in the actual artifacts, so he had no trouble buying them up," said Owena. "We have quite an extensive collection now. I'm determined to keep his memory alive by continuing his work."

The foundation offices were housed behind the museum that displayed its collection. In the laboratory area, technical assistants worked at all sorts of jobs connected to the treasure. Some were cataloging the various artifacts—coins, statues, gold and silver plates. Others were busy cleaning silver utensils, goblets, and other items.

"Salt water corrodes silver, but leaves gold untarnished," explained Owena. "That's why gold is comparatively easy to spot on the ocean floor."

"I read that there are almost as many ships waiting to be found as have already been discovered," said Cassie. "Is that true?"

"Probably," Owena replied. "A high percentage of ships that set out for Spain never made it. And treasure-hunting is still a young business."

Owena led them over to a long table. "Here's a stack of photos you might enjoy looking over," she said. "They show many of the artifacts that Whit has found. Todd is careful to make a photographic record of every artifact even if it is being shipped out of Florida. And in this scrapbook are a number of the magazine articles Todd has written."

Cassie flipped through the book of clippings. "It must be good for Todd's professional image to have all these articles with his name on them," she remarked.

"He is a bit of a newshound," said Owena, with an understanding smile. "But then he's very good at what he does."

"Especially for one so young," added Alex.

"One doesn't have to be old to be an expert in a field." Owena winked at Cassie.

Cassie smiled and returned her attention to the articles. One in particular had caught her eye. It was about the gold jaguar that was supposed to have been on board the *Madreperla*. Intended for the queen of Spain, it had taken countless hours of work to create and was, of course, the only one of its kind. Those who had seen it pronounced it one of the most exquisite pieces of gold sculpture ever made. There was an artist's sketch of the piece that took Cassie's breath away.

"Nice, isn't it?" said a deep voice behind her.

Cassie turned to see Todd Wrightson watching her read the article. "It certainly is," agreed Cassie. "Do you think you'll ever see the real thing?"

"Absolutely," Todd answered without hesitation. "Whit has to be very close to the site of the main treasure by now. We've found so many clues that there's no doubt. It's only a matter of time."

"Why do you think someone's trying to slow him down, Todd?" asked Cassie. "What would be a motive for vandalizing his boats and equipment?"

Todd shrugged. "Maybe someone else is looking. Secretly. There are plenty of smugglers down here—pirates, you could call them."

Owena overheard Todd's remark. "There have been pirates in this area ever since there have been ships," she said. "No doubt they've even caused some of the original shipwrecks themselves. And once a wreck is found, tight security has to be maintained day and night. There are plenty of renegade divers who'll try to steal a share of the treasure."

"Could someone else have already found the treasure ship?" Cassie asked, thinking out loud.

"It's conceivable," said Todd, "but not probable. It would have to be someone who knew what Whit was doing."

"And with the know-how to be one step ahead of him," Cassie added.

"Right." Todd laughed. "You're pretty sharp'ror a tourist, Cassandra. Are you sure you aren't a treasure hunter in disguise?"

Cassie looked at Todd to make sure he was just teasing. She couldn't tell.

"You were there when I nearly drowned yesterday," Cassie reminded him. "Did I look like an experienced treasure hunter?"

She laughed and Todd joined her. "I'm having a small party at my apartment this evening, Cassandra," he said, changing the subject. "Why don't you and Alex come? I have a few nice artifacts of my own. In fact, most of my salary goes to my collection."

"Thanks for the invitation," Cassie answered. "We'll be there." She would very much like to see Todd Wrightson's apartment. The more she knew about the suspects in this case, the better.

But was Todd a suspect? she asked herself. Of course, every member of the crew was. But surely his obsession with the jaguar statue would make him the last one to prevent Whit from finding it.

"In fact," Todd went on, "why don't you come for dinner, too? Keir and I have decided to cook up a batch of shrimp before the party. Keir makes a hot sauce that'll light up your eyes and clear the cobwebs from your brain."

"Great," said Alex, who had joined them. "We make a smashing salad, and Cassie has an old family recipe for dressing."

"I do?" asked Cassie, startled.

"Well, one of us has to," said Alex, laughing, "and it isn't me." Cassie supposed that with the staff of servants on the Bennett family's estate, Alex never even went near the kitchen.

The girls agreed that they would bring the salad fixings to Todd's later that evening.

Cassie, Alex, and Owena were still talking about treasure-hunting when they returned to Owena's boat. The last thing they were thinking of was more trouble.

But trouble was waiting for them.

Taped to the rearview mirror was a note. Cassie quickly tore it off and saw that it was obviously intended for her.

Reading it made her feel as though she were suffocating all over again. It said:

STOP STICKING YOUR NOSE INTO SOMETHING THAT DOESN'T CONCERN YOU. NEXT TIME YOU MAY NOT BE SO LUCKY. BREATHING SHOULD NEVER BE TAKEN FOR GRANTED.

*C*assie tore the note off the mirror and studied it closely. The words were scrawled in childish block letters, obviously to disguise the author's handwriting.

"Can you tell anything about the person who sent this threat, Cassandra?" asked Alex.

"No, I can't," said Cassie curtly. She looked at Alex and Owena. "There's something else that should never be taken for granted—being able to scare off a detective this easily."

That evening, with a bag of lettuce, spinach, tomatoes, fresh mushrooms, and broccoli, the girls followed the directions Todd had given them to his apartment house near the marina.

"I hope I didn't forget anything for the dressing," said Cassie, counting house numbers.

"Maybe our host will have it if you did forget something," said Alex.

The girls had had time for a quick change at Owena's before coming back to Key West. Alex looked festive in a red-and-turquoise patterned skirt. Cassie had slipped into another one of Alex's outfits, a red Indian print dress. Her long silver earrings jangled as they walked along.

Todd met the girls at the door and led them into his small kitchen, where Keir was already busy with the dinner preparations.

"Want to help?" Keir asked, as Cassie set her groceries down on the counter.

"What are you doing?" Cassie asked.

Keir had a big pot of water boiling on the stove. He was bending over a bucket in the sink and occasionally throwing something onto a sheet of newspaper on the counter.

"Popping the heads off the shrimp." Keir grinned, a mischievous twinkle in his eyes.

"I'd better stick to the salad," Cassie said, laughing.

In no time at all the four sat down at a small table to make a meal of shrimp, garlic bread, and a huge tossed salad topped with Cassie's homemade French dressing. Keir's shrimp sauce was as fiery as Todd had promised.

"Old Jamaican recipe," Keir said, taking the hard

casing off a shrimp and dipping it into the pool of red sauce on his plate.

Todd put a reggae cassette on the tapedeck to get them all in the party mood. Soon other divers started showing up, ready to dance. Cassie hoped a lot of people would be at the party. She knew it would be easier to snoop around if there were a crowd.

"Let me show you my rare fish," Todd said, coming up behind Cassie after dinner. He put his hand under her elbow and escorted her to the den.

Two huge fish tanks dominated the room. "This is an elephant fish," Todd said, pointing to one with a long nose. "They're expensive and hard to find. My favorite in this tank, though, is the African polka-dot catfish."

"Is it rare, too?" Cassie asked. She liked the lavender-colored fish, which was indeed covered with white polka dots. It swam upside down, appearing to look at them.

"Yes, it's rare." Todd moved to the other tank. "These are Siamese tiger fish. They're expensive, but not terribly rare."

While Cassie was still looking at the aquarium, Todd went to help Keir find more glasses.

One of Todd's friends stopped by the tank and peered into the greenish water. "Wow, these fish are great!" she exclaimed. "Todd is a fanatic about rare things. Have you seen his book collection?"

When Cassie shook her head, the girl went on, "It's in the library. You ought to go have a look."

"Maybe I will," said Cassie. She walked down the hall to the library.

The room was lined with books from floor to ceiling. So many art objects and artifacts caught her eye, though, that Cassie did no more than glance at the books. There were silver goblets, all sorts of old coins, and a stone statue she recognized as pre-Colombian.

These must be worth a fortune, she thought. They must cost more than Todd can afford unless he has family money. She knew that Whit couldn't pay his employees much—if anything—these days.

She looked furtively around. Todd was still nowhere in sight, so she decided to investigate further.

She pulled open the drawer of an old table located on one side of the room. There she found a small gold platter, a gold buckle, and a clump of heavily encrusted silver that hadn't yet been cleaned.

Behind her someone softly cleared his throat.

"Enjoying the rest of my collection?" Todd asked. His smile had a funny twist. "I haven't had time to clean those up and display them."

"Oh, I'm sorry, Todd. I'm just naturally nosy, I guess."

"Yes, I suppose you are, considering that's part of your job."

"What—what do you mean?" asked Cassie.

"You're not a tourist, are you, Cassandra? Tourists don't ask the kind of questions you ask. And most of them don't snoop around in people's houses."

"Oh, well, I—"

"But detectives do, don't they?" Todd stepped closer to Cassie.

Her cover was blown. Todd knew who she really was!

Taken aback, Cassie tried to collect her thoughts.

Suddenly Todd threw his head back and laughed heartily. "Cassandra! Don't look so upset. I was just kidding!" He took her arm and led her back to the party. "I hope you didn't find anything that will incriminate me," he said jokingly.

"Nothing serious," answered Cassie, smiling and tossing her head in what she hoped was a casual manner. Some detective I am, Cassie thought as she and Todd began to dance.

Soon after, Cassie decided she'd done enough investigating for one night. She and Alex had promised Owena they'd meet her back at the boat at ten o'clock, so they took their leave. As they walked back to the marina, Cassie filled her friend in on the events of the evening.

"Todd seems to have taken your snooping very calmly," said Alex.

"Perhaps even too calmly, considering how obsessed he is with his things," said Cassie. "But what really interests me is where he gets the money to pay for them. Do you know whether he's inherited money from his family?"

"I have no idea," answered Alex. "But he strikes me as the sort of man who will always find a way to get what he wants."

The girls headed back to the marina early again the next morning. Alex wanted to do some background research on the lesser known patrons of the foundation who were coming to the party; Cassie wanted to go back through Whit's records. Part of her plan was to look over the dates and places of the incidents of vandalism. She wanted to compare them with the dive sites and with the type of small finds that had been made on each site. Was there any connection? For instance, did all the vandalism occur when a boat was scheduled for one particular site or immediately after a certain type of artifact was salvaged? There was a piece missing in this puzzle, and she needed to find it.

At the marina, Alex and Cassie made plans to meet for lunch and went their separate ways. Cassie had called Whit before coming, only to be informed that he wouldn't be available because he was taking out the *Whitewater*. But he'd told Cassie where he kept the hidden key to his office on the *Riptide*.

When she arrived at Whit's office, however, she found the door ajar. Didn't he say he'd be gone by the time Cassie got there? The *Whitewater* was out of the harbor. She'd checked when she passed its mooring.

Quietly she pushed the door half-way open and looked in. The office seemed empty. Still, she couldn't be sure. To avoid a trap, she slowly took one step forward and peered into the cabin.

Blam! Someone shoved the door at her, hard. Cassie stumbled sideways and fell against Whit's desk. By the time she scrambled to her feet, the intruder had run out the door, slamming it behind him.

Cassie yanked the door open and ran out onto the deck. The intruder was still on the boat, and turned around when he heard her coming. For a moment their eyes met. Then he swung himself over the side of the boat and took off down the dock. When he stopped to pick up the cap that had sailed off his head, Cassie got a better look at him.

He was quite tall, with a full beard and reddish hair that showed in startling contrast to his deep, almost black, tan. Like everyone else on Key West, he was wearing a medallion of some sort around his neck. It swung out from his chest when he bent over and gleamed gold in the early morning sun.

By the time Cassie had jumped off the boat to follow him, she had lost sight of the intruder. The docks were completely empty, except for an old man dozing on one of the many wooden benches facing the ocean. She guessed the intruder must have ducked onto a boat about a dozen moorings down, but which one?

On impulse, she approached the old man and asked him if he'd seen anyone run by a moment ago.

"Aye, that would be the captain of the *Sea Hawk*, that would," answered the old man. "He took off like the Furies were after him and went back on board his own ship.

"He's a great one for the ladies," he added with a wink after Cassie had thanked him. "You watch your step now!"

I will, thought Cassie as she headed toward the ship. Believe me, I will.

The *Sea Hawk* was a bright green vessel, obviously newly painted and refurbished. A sign posted on the dock advertised tours every evening at eight o'clock. Those interested were advised to sign up for a tour at Key West Visitors Center.

I'll just have to go on board, thought Cassie. If I don't, I won't find out why the captain of the *Sea Hawk* was in Whit's office.

She tiptoed up the gangplank, her tennis shoes noiseless on the old wooden boards. Once on deck she proceeded as quietly as possible. If anyone stopped her, she would ask about the tours. But no one did. She made one full pass around the deck, then decided to go below.

Softly she slipped down the steps. They opened into a small, neat galley. Taking a fast look around, she tiptoed farther into the dim interior.

First she entered a tiny room with four bunks attached to the walls. Then she opened the door of a tiny bathroom. One more doorway opened onto the hall. Cassie stopped and listened. Still nothing.

Holding her breath, Cassie stepped across the sill of the last doorway and entered another cabin. It was an office, with two bunks built into one wall and a desk built into the other.

Hastily, she rifled through the papers on the desk. There were passenger lists, menus for take-out food, a tide schedule—and finally, the evidence she was looking for.

In her hand Cassie held a sonar reading stamped with the name of Whit's company, *Tesoros Hallados*. Glancing over the sonar reading, she saw that it was a reading of an area of ocean near an island called Oyster Key.

This must be what the thief had taken from Whit's office, Cassie concluded. But why was Oyster Key so important?

There was only one way to find out. She slipped the paper into the pocket of her shorts and made her way back up the stairs as quickly as possible.

She congratulated herself on a successful mission. With this evidence, she would be able to stop whoever had been vandalizing Whit's boats and equipment. Then he would find the *Madreperla*, and . . .

A blow to the back of her head sent Cassie reeling. The last thing she saw before blacking out was half a gold doubloon, swinging above her head.

Then she sailed into space.

*T*he ocean was cold. Sputtering, Cassie regained consciousness in the waters off the stern of the *Sea Hawk*.

She floundered around for a bit, but soon got her bearings and swam to the dock. Hauling herself onto the boards, she sat for a moment waiting for her mind to clear.

Someone must have been watching her the whole time she was on the *Sea Hawk*. It had been foolish of her to assume she was alone. You call this being careful? she chided herself.

Who had thrown her overboard? She tried to remember what had happened just before she'd landed in the water. Someone had hit her over the head, and then . . .

The half doubloon! She'd recognize that anywhere. It had been Keir Gardner who had attacked her!

"Oh no," Cassie whispered aloud. "Not Keir."

She wished she was mistaken about the doubloon. Maybe it had been some trick of the light. And yet she had good reason to suspect that Keir had smashed Whit's sonar. And he could be violent when provoked.

Were Keir and the captain of the *Sea Hawk* partners in crime? Cassie decided to ask the old sailor on the bench a few questions about the red-haired captain. Then she saw that the bench was empty.

I'll have to find another way to investigate the *Sea Hawk*, thought Cassie. Well, at least I got Whit's property back for him. She pulled the stolen sonar reading out of her pocket and looked at it. It was a soggy mess.

Sighing, she got up and went back along the dock to the *Riptide*. Luckily, she carried a towel and her bathing suit in her duffel. When she reached the cabin, she changed and hung her wet T-shirt and shorts on the deck to dry.

Then she set to work. Whit kept meticulous records of each dive site: its location, when he had worked it, and what he had found there. But after an hour of poring over maps and schedules, Cassie still could find no connection between the sites and the vandalism. Nor could she figure out from the records why someone would find a sonar reading of the area near Oyster Key so important.

When Alex came to get Cassie for lunch, she found her friend still hunched over the desk.

"Cassie, what happened to you?" she asked, noticing Cassie's wet hair and bathing suit. "You look as if you've already gone swimming."

"It wasn't recreational, I'm afraid," said Cassie. She related her adventure of the morning, leaving out only the part about the half doubloon. She didn't want to implicate Keir without direct evidence.

"Alex, there's something going on here besides the vandalism," Cassie finished. "And it has to do with the captain of the *Sea Hawk*. But I haven't been able to put all the pieces together yet. I'm waiting for the next one to fall into place."

"Well, while you're waiting, let's go get some lunch," Alex suggested. "Even detectives have to eat, you know!"

Cassie pulled her damp shorts back over her bathing suit and left with Alex for a lunch of tacos and refried beans. By the time they returned to the office, Whit was sitting behind his desk.

"I see you've spent a busy morning," said the treasure hunter, indicating the piles of paper Cassie had sorted through on his desk. "Find anything?"

"I'm not sure," said Cassie, unwilling to elaborate until she could present Whit with more definite proof. "Whit," she asked, "if someone were keeping a close watch on your dives, do you think there's a chance they could find the *Madreperla* before you?''

"I can't conceive of it. And they wouldn't have the permit to salvage it.'' Whit pulled out a pipe and began to fill it with fragrant tobacco.

"Couldn't they dive when you weren't in the area and secretly remove some of the treasure?'' Cassie asked.

"They'd have to work at night,'' Whit replied. "I suppose it's possible, but not very likely. Only after an outfit like *Tesoros Hallados* does all the searching, the hard work of finding a wreck, do the smugglers come out in droves. That's why we either dive day and night or keep night watch on important sites.'' Whit looked at Cassie sharply. "What makes you think that's a possibility? Have you found any proof?''

"Well, no, but—'' Cassie began.

"Then don't start giving me ideas. I've got enough to worry about,'' Whit complained. "The winch on the *Whitewater* broke down again.''

"More vandalism?'' asked Alex.

"No, just a normal malfunction. But that's the winch that was tinkered with earlier. I thought we'd fixed it.'' Whit made an impatient gesture. "Just when I wanted to get back to work at Oyster Key.'' He gave a long pull on his pipe.

"Oyster Key?'' asked Cassie.

"That's where—where Paolo drowned,'' said

Whit. "I'd taken some sonar readings of the area before the storm."

"Have you told anyone you were going back to Oyster Key?" asked Cassie.

"Sure. Everyone knows—well, the whole crew." Whit turned back to the papers on his desk. "Listen, girls, after I fix that winch I'm going to be working late tonight. If you want a lift back to the island, I'll be here till ten. Just let me know."

"Thanks a lot, Whit," Alex answered. Owena had dropped them at the marina earlier with instructions to call when they wanted a ride.

Cassie hesitated. Should she tell Whit about the stolen sonar reading now? No, not until she could prove *why* it was stolen.

"Come on, Alex, let's go," she whispered to her friend. "I have an idea." They started out the door.

Then Cassie remembered something. "Whit," she said casually, "was Keir with you on the *Whitewater* today? We were hoping to, uh, maybe go to the movies with him later."

"No, haven't seen him all day," answered Whit, without looking up. "He told me he had pressing personal business."

Pressing personal business? Cassie thought grimly. I think I know what that business might be.

The clerk behind the information booth at the Key West Visitors Center was friendly and eager to help.

"Night tours on the *Sea Hawk*?" she said, reaching into her desk and taking out a laminated schedule. "Let's see. Yes, they leave the marina every night at eight o'clock sharp. They specialize in night diving. You bring the bathing suit, they provide all the scuba gear."

"Do you know where they're diving tonight?" Cassie pressed her.

"Oyster Key," the clerk answered. "There's a beautiful coral reef there, I hear. It's a great place to see octopi and other shy night creatures."

"Thanks a lot for the information," Cassie said, beaming at her. "You've been a great help."

"Don't you want a ticket?" called out the disappointed clerk. But Cassie was already hurrying Alex out of the Visitors Center.

"What was that all about?" asked Alex, who had listened to the exchange with growing excitement.

Cassie knew she was hot on the trail now. "The captain of the *Sea Hawk* steals Whit's sonar reading of Oyster Key, and tonight the *Sea Hawk* is taking tourists diving at Oyster Key."

"You're saying it's no coincidence, Cassandra?"

"Precisely. Ready for some adventure?"

"I guess I am. What do you have in mind?" Alex asked.

"We're going night diving."

"Cassie, you don't have much day experience," Alex objected. "And I've never dived at night."

96

"Whoever stole that sonar reading must be connected with the vandalism incidents," Cassie said urgently. "And we have to find out why he stole the reading and make sure he doesn't damage any more of Whit's equipment."

"You're right, Cassie. So we're going on the tour boat?"

"No, we're going to follow it," Cassie corrected her. "To Oyster Key. Something is happening there, and we're going to find out what it is.

"But first we need some gear, and a means of transportation," Cassie went on. "I'd like to find a guide who knows the Keys well. We don't want to get out into the ocean and lose our way."

"No, we certainly don't," said Alex nervously. "Maybe I know someone who can help us. Come on."

The girls walked toward the marina.

"I hope he's still here. He waved to me at noon," Alex mumbled to herself. She hurried her friend down the pier until they came to a sign that read BOATS FOR RENT. Two boys sat on the dock, laughing and talking. One was picking out a tune on his guitar.

"Which one of you owns this business?" Alex asked.

"I do," said the younger of the two boys. He didn't look more than thirteen or fourteen. "Do you want to rent a boat for this afternoon?"

"Not this afternoon. Tonight," Cassie said. She looked at the boats the boy had for rent. They were old and their paint was peeling. One had a tattered canvas awning.

The boy followed her glance. "We may not have money for frills," he said. "But I can guarantee good service. The best," he added.

Cassie smiled. Only the "best" will do, she reminded herself. She liked this boy's brash salesmanship. "Okay," said Cassie, "you're hired."

"I'm your man," said the boy, standing up. His friend smiled, gave him the thumbs-up sign, and left.

"Do you know these waters well?" Cassie asked the boy. She wanted to make sure he was as capable as he sounded.

"My family are fishermen," the boy said proudly. "We've been fishing the Keys for generations."

"So you know where Oyster Key is?" Cassie continued to question him.

"Of course. Is that where you want to go?" The boy looked eager.

"Yes, it is. Do you have diving equipment we can rent? And lights?" Cassie asked.

"My brother and I dive. But I don't have a license to take divers out."

"I'll take that responsibility," Cassie said, looking him straight in the eye. "Let's say you had a couple

of friends who liked to dive. You'd all go diving together, wouldn't you?"

The boy smiled. He understood her reasoning.

"My name's Mannie, friends. Have you ever
dived at night?"

"No, but we're dying to try it," said Cassie.

"Don't say that word, Cassie," warned Alex.

"Tonight, then," Mannie said. He spread his
arms as if to welcome them to the wonderful world
of night diving.

"Tonight," Cassie echoed him. They left Mannie
with a deposit and agreed to meet him back at the
boat at eight o'clock.

By now it was late afternoon, four hours before
the night's adventure would begin. Cassie persuaded Alex to take in a showing of *The Maltese Fal-
con* at the local second-run movie house. She'd
already seen it five times herself, but she wanted to
share one of her favorite movies with her friend.
Then they ate a quick dinner at the coffee shop and
went back to the *Riptide* so Alex could change into
her bathing suit.

Whit wasn't there, so Cassie left him a note asking for a ride back to the island with him later that
evening. Then they went back to Mannie's.

He was waiting for them at the pier. I hope Mannie's diving gear is in better condition than his boat,
Cassie thought as she and Alex climbed into the battered runabout.

To their surprise, the boat kicked over the first time and hummed into action. "I'm a good mechanic," said Mannie, reading the girls' minds. "Are you ready to go?"

"I want you to follow that boat," said Cassie, pointing to the *Sea Hawk*. The tour boat was well ahead of them, already pulling out of the bay. "Stay far behind, so they don't know we're here."

"Follow that boat, like on TV?" Mannie gave a delighted laugh. "Danger, action, excitement, right?"

"There could be a lot of danger, Mannie," Cassie warned him.

"That's okay," he said. "I've watched a lot of TV. I've seen a lot of dangerous action."

"This is not TV, Mannie," Alex reminded him. "This is real."

"That's even better. *Real* danger." Mannie gave a small whoop as he steered the runabout out of the marina and into the open water.

Cassie grinned. Mannie's excitement was contagious. She could already feel the adrenaline pumping through her body.

It didn't take long for her to realize that Mannie was going to be indispensable to them. She and Alex would never have been able to navigate the waters off Key West without someone who knew the area well.

About a half hour later they came to a stop off

Oyster Key. They had pulled as close as they dared to the tour boat, where the tourists were preparing for their dive.

Cassie and Alex had taken advantage of the ride to put on Mannie's diving equipment and test it. Now they sat silently, waiting for the time to go overboard.

Shouting and splashing, the divers from the tour boat went over the side and into the water. Cassie and Alex lowered themselves into the rocking waves as quietly as possible. In the dark of the night, they swam as close as they could to the group in the water. When the group leader gave the signal to dive, Cassie and Alex went under.

Following the divers wasn't hard. It was rather like chasing fireflies in the darkness. But Cassie felt as though she were swimming in a giant pool of ink. Her thoughts wandered. Did sharks swim at night? Fran had told them that sharks were generally more curious than aggressive. Still, bumping into one at night might be considered an attack from the shark's point of view.

And then there were rays and other dangerous creatures. Cassie wished she could turn on the light she carried, even for a few seconds. But she didn't dare.

Swimming quickly, the pair followed close on the heels, or rather the flippers, of the group of divers. When four men dropped back, Cassie gave Alex's hand a hard squeeze. She prayed the divers weren't going to turn around and swim toward them.

Instead, the four veered off to the right. The girls followed, guided by the large searchlights the divers carried. Within a few hundred yards, the divers came to a halt beside a wall of coral and flooded the area with lights.

Cassie motioned for Alex to stop. Not until the divers looked totally engrossed in their task did the girls move in closer.

Before them was an incredible sight. Cassie blinked her eyes once, shut them, and opened them again.

The divers were loading nets with pure gold!

Even though Cassie had seen gold treasure in the museum, there was something magical about seeing it down here on the ocean floor. Gold really *didn't* tarnish in the salt water, not even after lying on the bottom of the ocean for hundreds of years. And if this gold had come from the *Madreperla*, it had been here for *four* hundred years. The gold bars looked bright and shiny—the way they must have been when the Spaniards had melted down the gold and molded it into shape.

Was this gold from Whit's treasure ship? Were these divers smuggling? Surely they were using the tourist boat to hide the real reason for their night dive.

Cassie was finding it difficult to stay in one place.

She kept waving her flippers, wishing she had something to hang onto. Without meaning to, she floated closer to the activity than she'd planned.

Thump! Something bumped her arm, hard. Her reaction was as automatic as it would have been in a dark room. She switched on the light to see what had run into her.

The silent shadow moved on, obviously not a threat. But her light had alerted the divers. She saw one of them look up and spot her immediately. She saw him nudge his friend.

And when they started after her, she saw that each of them carried a deadly spear gun!

*M*aking her best under-
water turn ever, Cassie spun around and swam for
her life. She hoped that Alex was right behind her.
Maybe their head start would enable them to outwit
the smugglers. She knew the coral formations were
often large and offered many small nooks and cran-
nies to hide in.

Choosing not to use her light to avoid being seen,
Cassie swam in the dark water. She felt she had lost
her sense of direction. The dark wall of water
seemed to close in, smothering her. For the first time
she understood Todd's fear of diving. She was be-
coming claustrophobic.

In desperation she flashed on her light. What dif-
ference could it make? The divers following them
had lights, too.

The beam illuminated a path directly in front of her and Alex. Then Alex switched on her larger spotlight as well. Just ahead loomed a wall of coral. Cassie swerved and followed it.

She glanced back to make sure that Alex was behind her and caught sight of the two divers in the distance. In the split second that their light was out of her eyes, she saw that one of them seemed huge and misshapen, almost monstrous.

If those divers caught up to the girls, she and Alex would be no match for them.

Just as Cassie was losing hope, she spotted an opening in the coral. It was tiny, almost window-like. But it seemed their only chance.

Stretching her arms out in front of her, Cassie kicked her feet and let herself glide through the hole. She was careful not to snag her scuba hoses on the razor-sharp edges around her.

She was in a maze. Immediately the coral branched out into two corridors. Cassie chose one and led the way down the narrow corridor. She tried not to think about how she and Alex would get back out if their lights failed. Turning and twisting, the passage seemed to go on forever. Suddenly it opened into what seemed like a large room.

Cassie stopped abruptly, and Alex bumped into her from behind. Before their eyes, a startled octopus jetted through one of the three exits from the coral room, a cloud of dark ink spraying out behind it. Hoping she was making the right choice, Cassie swam through the opening to the right and turned off her light. Alex did the same.

They were just in time to see a lone diver enter the room, hesitate, and take the exit to the left.

His wrong guess might give them just enough time to get away.

Snapping on her light again, Cassie continued forward. She wondered what had happened to the huge diver. Had he run into a deadly sea creature? Had he given up the chase and gone back to retrieve more gold? Or did he know where the passage of coral led? Maybe he would be waiting for them at the other end.

If they ever reached the other end. Cassie tried to push back the thought that they were irretrievably lost. She had one comfort, at any rate. She had solved part of the mystery that had brought her to the Keys.

Now she knew that someone was taking treasure illegally from one of the sites Whit himself would soon explore. The incidents of vandalism must have been intended to keep Whit busy elsewhere.

And she had found out who was involved in the smuggling operation. The captain of the *Sea Hawk*. And perhaps Keir.

Cassie was so lost in thought that she nearly swam into the large shadowy figure looming before her. It was a manta ray, at least nine feet across, with four lethal prongs of poison in its long tail.

Alex tugged at her arm, and the two girls swam in place while the manta floated on ahead. Though Cassie knew that mantas weren't deadly to humans, she didn't want a close encounter with one of its stingers.

The manta did give Cassie hope that the tunnel was coming to an end. Perhaps it would lead them out of the maze.

And so it did. Following the ray at a safe distance, the girls soon found themselves in open water again. Grabbing Alex's arm, Cassie pointed upward. In a few minutes, they had kicked their way to the surface of the ocean.

Cassie spit out her mouthpiece and breathed in the cool night air. "Where are we?" she whispered. "I can't even see the stars. I can hardly tell where the sky stops and the ocean begins."

It was the blackest night Cassie had ever seen. A fog seemed to have settled over the water. Was it her imagination or had the sea grown rougher while they were underwater? Salt water kept slapping her face, stinging her eyes.

"We're lost, Cassie," said Alex, her teeth chattering. "And I'm freezing."

"Me, too." Cassie started to shake, only partly from the cold.

They fell silent. In the quiet of the night, Cassie's

ears could pick up every tiny sound around them. Finally she heard something besides the splash of water.

"Listen! Do you hear that?" said Cassie. She tried to pin down the direction of the faint laughter and shouting that carried across the water. "It's the night diving party returning to their boat." She listened again. "Come on, Alex, this way."

In the fog, the girls couldn't see the ship, so they had to rely on following the sounds. Cassie swam on the surface of the water, pulling her mask over her face to keep the water out of her eyes. It would be faster to dive and swim under the waves, but she was afraid they'd lose their direction again.

When they got close enough to the *Sea Hawk* to see it through the fog, they heard the engine start up. Then they watched it slowly cut through the water and leave.

"Okay, our own boat has to be somewhere nearby. Do we dare yell to Mannie?" said Cassie.

"Let's wait just a few minutes," Alex cautioned. "Remember how their voices carried over the water. I don't want to be faced with those spear guns again."

Cassie felt impatient. She wanted to follow the *Sea Hawk* back to the marina and watch the smugglers unload their cargo—not just the tourists, but the gold bars she knew they were carrying.

Had the smugglers continued to steal after they'd

given up on chasing Cassie and Alex? she wondered. Or had they settled for what they could carry in one load tonight? They must realize that if Cassie escaped and reported their activity, their operation was over.

Cassie felt as if she and Alex had been underwater for hours. She'd bet that in that time the divers had worked furiously, bringing up as many loads as they could.

She had to get back to Key West.

"Mannie!" Cassie called out into the darkness. "Mannie! Can you hear me? Where are you?"

There was no answer. The silence broken, Alex joined in the shouting. But they heard no voice besides their own.

"Where is he?" Cassie wondered.

"You don't suppose he would leave us here and go back alone, do you?" asked Alex in a worried tone.

"No, of course not." But Cassie was worried, too. What if they'd made a mistake in trusting Mannie? After all, his small business wasn't far from where the *Sea Hawk* was moored. What if the captain paid him just a little to keep his eyes open? With his vivid imagination, Mannie might enjoy a little sabotage work. . . .

Now *you're* imagining things, Cassie told herself. But where was Mannie?

She couldn't see past her nose in this fog. Cassie

stopped treading water and started to backstroke gently, looking all around her.

Clunk! "Ouch," Cassie yelped, spinning around.

"I think you've found what we were looking for," said Alex, swimming over. "The hard way." She pushed the runabout away from Cassie and pulled herself up. "Where's Mannie?" she asked. "He's not on board."

"You don't think—" Cassie began. She jumped for the side of the boat, grabbed the edge, and bellied over, tumbling into the passenger's seat.

Mannie *was* there. But he was slumped over the steering wheel, out cold. Or worse—dead.

"**M**annie!" Cassie cried. She dumped her tank, flinging the harness off her shoulders. Quickly she leaned over and placed her fingers on the carotid artery in Mannie's neck. His pulse was strong and getting stronger.

"Ohhh," he groaned, clutching his head. "He hit me before I could stop him."

"Before you could stop who? Who hit you?" asked Cassie. Alex dipped an old towel in the water, wrung it out, and gave it to Mannie.

"I don't know who," the boy said, pressing the cool towel against his head. "He was wearing a mask. He didn't say anything, just hit me." Mannie winced from the pain. "Nobody seems to get hurt this bad on TV," he grumbled.

"That bump on your head is real, Mannie," said

Cassie. "TV is only pretend." Cassie wished she had dry clothes to put on. She was even colder out of the water. "Let's get back to Key West. We can find a doctor if you think you need one, or take you to the hospital. We need to be sure you don't have a concussion."

"I have a bad headache, but I'm okay," Mannie said gamely.

"Do you think you can pilot the boat back to Key West?" asked Alex. "Or I can pilot if you'll navigate."

"I'm all right," Mannie insisted. He sat up in the driver's seat and pressed the ignition to start the engine. Nothing happened. "What—" He tried again.

The small craft tossed back and forth in the waves. Holding on to the side of the boat, Cassie worked her way back to the engine. She was afraid she knew what had happened. Experts at vandalism could stop a boat easily.

Mannie followed Cassie to the stern. "Hold the light," he instructed. Cassie focused her flashlight on the small engine.

Removing the cover, Mannie took one look and groaned again.

"What is it? Are you all right?" Cassie asked.

"I am. This engine isn't. Now I know why I was hit on the head. Someone wants us to stay right here all night."

"What do you mean?" Cassie asked.

"The spark plug's gone," he explained. "See?" Cassie looked to where his finger was pointing. The damage was obvious. Someone had ripped the plug out.

She slumped on the seat and looked around. Fortunately, the oars were still stacked against the side of the boat. "How long will it take us to row back to Key West, Mannie?" Cassie asked.

He considered. "In this chop? It would take three, maybe four hours in *good* weather."

"Sounds like a smashing way to spend the night," said Alex, sighing.

"We can't stay here all night," Cassie said firmly. How long would it be before they could tell Whit about their discovery? The smugglers could be in Mexico by morning. "Think, everyone, think!"

"Maybe we're in luck," said Mannie suddenly, scrambling back to one of the seats. "They didn't take my tool box. Now if only I remembered to put in an extra spark plug."

Again Cassie held the light for Mannie. "How about that?" she said, pointing to the part.

"You're right." Mannie laughed triumphantly. "The bad guys lose again."

He bent over the engine. "Try the ignition," he called to Alex, who had moved to the front of the boat.

The engine growled, complained, and then kicked over. Alex fed it more gas to keep it running.

"Hurrah!" shouted Cassie over the wind.

"Can we go home now?" asked Alex. "This ocean cruise has lost its charm."

The ride back to Key West was like being on a bucking horse. The small boat bounced and pitched in the waves, but at least it kept going. Finally, bruised and battered, the threesome maneuvered the runabout into the harbor where Mannie tied it securely.

"Thanks, Mannie," said Alex, handing him a generous tip over the fee he'd quoted earlier.

"Are you sure you don't want us to take you to the hospital?" asked Cassie. "You really ought to have that bump looked at."

"I'm fine now," Mannie said. He gave them a thumbs-up sign and a big grin. "Thanks for the adventure. If you ever need help again, you know where to find me."

"We sure do," said Cassie, shaking the boy's hand. "Bye, Mannie."

She and Alex hurried down the dock. "We're hours late," said Cassie. "Whit must be worried sick."

Whit was pacing the deck of the *Riptide*, puffing on his pipe, when he saw Cassie and Alex. "Where have you been? You've kept me and Fran waiting all night—" He took a good look at at the bedraggled girls. "Come on inside. It's going to rain any minute. I just put on a fresh pot of coffee." Whit sounded relieved. Cassie could tell how worried he'd been.

"We had a little underwater run-in with your competition, Whit," Cassie began, warming her hands on the sides of a steaming mug of coffee.

"You went diving at night?" asked Fran, coming fully awake. "With your lack of experience? That was such a dangerous thing to do, Cassandra!"

"Yes, but a necessary one," Cassie answered. "We followed a tourist boat to Oyster Key." Cassie pointed to the map on the wall of the cabin. "We went down right about here."

"What were you thinking of?" Whit said. He sounded almost angry.

"Whit, I didn't tell you earlier," said Cassie, "but this morning I discovered a man in your office looking through your papers. He stole a sonar reading of the area around Oyster Key."

"Just this morning I announced that we'd be going back to work at Oyster Key," Whit said wonderingly.

"Yes," said Cassie, "and I think that announcement made someone determined to get ahold of the sonar reading."

"But I didn't tell anyone except my crew," said Whit. "How could he have known?"

"I don't know yet," said Cassie. The statement was only half true. But she wasn't ready to tell anybody her suspicion about Keir. Not yet.

117

"Anyway," she continued, "this man is the captain of the *Sea Hawk*. When we found out that the *Sea Hawk* was taking tourists out to dive off Oyster Key tonight, we decided to follow them. And we found divers pulling up gold bars."

"Gold bars? Off Oyster Key?" asked Whit excitedly. He looked closely at the spot on the wall map that Cassie had pointed out. "Are you sure?"

"It's hard to mistake pure gold," said Alex. "The divers were lifting the bars in mesh nets and taking them up to the boat."

"The *Sea Hawk*'s tour business is just a disguise for its real business," said Cassie. "Smuggling. The smugglers must have destroyed your sonar and stolen that reading to keep you from working the area near Oyster Key while they finished the job," Cassie concluded.

The group was silent for a moment. "Could you tell how much gold was left to salvage?" Whit asked, sipping his coffee. He still seemed to be trying to take in the news.

"We didn't have time," Cassie said. "When the smugglers realized we were spying, they came after us with spear guns." She finished telling Whit and Fran about the rest of the night's adventures.

Fran had been strangely quiet during Cassie's revelations. Now, when the story was done, she got up and looked at the map. "So that's where it is," she mused, tracing her finger around Oyster Key. She shot Cassie a look full of bitterness. "And you're a detective."

"Quite a detective," said Whit. He shook his head. "I know I should be furious with you and Alex, Cassandra, for risking your lives like this. But I think you've found it. I really think you've found it." A big grin started to spread over his face.

"Found the *Madreperla*?" asked Cassie excitedly. "Your treasure?"

"I've spent all these years searching, with the best talent I could bring together. And it took a detective like you to find it," Whit said sincerely.

"Actually, the smugglers found it," Cassie pointed out. "But we found the smugglers."

"That's even better," said Whit. "You've led me to the richest treasure ship of my career!"

*C*assie stood at the railing of Whit's boat as it sped through the rain toward Sand Dollar Key. She felt exhausted, but satisfied. She knew there wasn't anything else she could do that night.

The *Sea Hawk* was not in her mooring at the marina. Whit had called the coast guard and warned them to keep an eye out for the ship.

The smugglers were probably hiding the gold somewhere. If the coast guard didn't find it aboard the ship, Cassie and Alex could only testify that divers from the boat were doing the stealing. The captain could deny any knowledge of it. He could still get away, since no one had seen the divers' faces.

Fran sat alone on the other side of the boat. After

121

the bitter look she had given Cassie earlier, Cassie knew something was troubling her.

Cassie sat down beside Whit's granddaughter. "What's the matter, Fran?" she asked. "Aren't you glad for your grandfather?"

Fran turned on her fiercely. "Why did you have to be the one to find that shipwreck?" she asked. "You're not the one who's been looking for it all these years."

Cassie guessed Fran's problem. "I was just the right person at the right time, I guess," she said.

Fran turned her head away. Cassie could hear her crying. "I'd always dreamed I'd find the *Madreperla* for my grandfather," the girl admitted in a softer tone. "It was one of the reasons I became a diver and went into marine biology. I wanted him to be proud of me."

"But your grandfather *is* proud of you," Cassie said sincerely. "I can hear it in his voice every time he speaks of you."

"I know he loves me," Fran said. "This was just something I wanted to do for him." She was silent for a moment, then added, "And I am happy for him. I'm just disappointed, that's all." She looked at Cassie and gave a short laugh. "Don't worry, Cassandra, I'll get over it." She got up and stood by the railing where Cassie had been a few minutes before. Obviously she wanted to be left alone.

Fran may be proud, Cassie thought. But at least

she's honest. She had the feeling that the next time they talked, Fran would be friendly again.

Cassie moved forward to the tiny cabin.

"Will you be able to dive tomorrow, Whit?" she asked. "To check out the wreck?"

"If this storm moves through, you can bet I'll be the first one down," Whit replied. He mancuvered his boat alongside Owena's dock. "I hope Owena isn't too worried about you two."

"She knows we were with you," said Alex.

"That probably made her worry all the more." Whit laughed. "If she's up, tell her the good news. That'll make her forget her worries. I'll fill her in tomorrow."

Cassie and Alex said good night to Whit and Fran and found the shell path up to Owena's house.

To the girls' surprise, Owena appeared to be asleep already. Maybe she thought they'd come home long before. Exhausted, each headed for a hot shower and bed.

Cassie lay still for a time in her comfortable bed, but she couldn't sleep. Her body was tired, but her mind was awake. Too awake.

She kept running through the events of the night: the dive, the discovery of the gold, the underwater chase. Something important was eluding her, but it wasn't clear in her mind.

Creak. She sat up in bed, listening. *Creak.* Someone was on the old wooden stairs. Then she heard footsteps coming down the hall. Throwing off her covers, Cassie got out of bed and cracked open the door.

She was just in time to see Keir's back as he disappeared into his mother's room. In half a minute he came out again and went back downstairs.

Keir! What was he doing here at this hour of the night? Cassie knew he had his own cabin by the edge of the ocean.

Cassie tiptoed to the railing and looked down. It was dark below. She moved quickly to Fidelia's room, listened, then pushed open the door, already ajar.

The cloth that covered the walls of Fidelia's room billowed out slightly as Cassie entered. Her senses were assaulted by the smell of strong incense.

But it was the small shrine on the table beside Fidelia's bed that caught Cassie's attention. A candle burned on either side of a photograph. The dish of incense burned with a small thread of smoke in front of the picture.

Cassie glanced behind her. She had no idea where Fidelia was, but Keir must have been looking for her. She moved closer to the bed, which had been slept in that night. Reaching out, she picked up the photo frame and stared at the picture.

This must be Paolo, she thought. He had the same dark, intense eyes as his mother and brother. The same eyes as—

Cassie shut her own eyes and willed herself to remember an image from yesterday. She covered the chin of the man in the photo and imagined him with reddish hair.

She caught her breath. Yes, the face was familiar. Paolo, Fidelia's dead son, was actually the man who had stolen the sonar reading from Whit's office. He was the captain of the *Sea Hawk*.

Suddenly everything became clear. So it hadn't been Keir who had thrown her overboard from the *Sea Hawk*. It had been his brother Paolo, who also wore half a gold doubloon around his neck.

Keir was innocent after all. Or was he? His brother was a thief, a smuggler. Was Keir his brother's accomplice?

Cassie knew what she had to do to find out.

The rain had stopped, and now light wisps of fog drifted across the sky like ghosts of the dead Spanish sailors. A crescent moon glimmered above, casting just enough light to see by.

Cassie followed Keir across Owena's soft, wet lawn. She had gone back to her room and pulled on jeans, a sweatshirt, and tennis shoes. Then she had hurried down the stairs and out of the house. She didn't want to lose him.

Keir's footsteps crunched on the seashell path down to the beach. Cassie followed as quietly as she could. When he headed along the sand in the direction of Treasure Beach, Cassie kept close to the thick bush that edged the sand. But Keir was moving so fast, he probably wouldn't notice that he was being followed.

Just as he came to the beach where they had swam the first day Cassie arrived, Keir veered off to the left. He followed the long narrow spit of land that curved around and formed Treasure Beach cove. At first Cassie thought there was no path, just a tangle of mangrove swamp.

It turned out that there was a passageway, but in the dark Cassie lost it several times. Limbs from the tangled mangrove slapped at her face and tore at her sweatshirt. Reaching out to push one large branch aside, she swallowed a scream. A snake dangled from the limb. She ducked down and quickly moved forward. What other creatures might be out here?

She had lost sight of Keir, but she knew there was only one way he could have gone. Eventually, he'd have to stop at the ocean. Her mind was full of questions. Above all, why was Keir coming out here in the middle of the night?

The path started to go slightly downhill. Cassie was about to follow it when she stopped abruptly at the sound of voices.

"Paolo, Paolo, is that really you?" cried Keir, sobbing.

"It is, little brother, it is," another voice said. "I'm sorry I had to pretend to be dead for so long. But wait till you see what I've got in the cave. We're leaving right now, you and me. We'll send for Mother as soon as we get settled."

"Leaving? Where are we going?" Keir asked.

"To Mexico," said the voice. "To live like kings. Come and see." The voices moved farther away.

They must be going to the cave that Paolo had mentioned, thought Cassie.

Below the hill where she stood, the moonlight shone in a path across the ocean. Anchored offshore was a ship, which had to be the *Sea Hawk*. Cassie could make out a small boat heading for the larger one.

Scrambling down the bank, she found the cave entrance and leaned in the shadows for a moment. Then, hearing no one, she slipped into the damp, musty-smelling hole. She wished she had a flashlight. She couldn't see a thing.

Without making a sound, she stepped farther inside. She stopped when she heard Keir say, "Paolo! All this gold? Where did you get it?"

"I found it. Pretty smart, wouldn't you say?"

Cassie peeked around the rock wall. There was a torch stuck in the dirt floor of the cave. It revealed a small stack of gold bars identical to those she'd seen the smugglers gathering from the ocean's floor.

"This is our last load," said Paolo. "The rest is on the ship already."

"The rest?" asked Keir. "How much do you

have?'' He sounded confused, as if uncertain how to react. He's just had a great shock, thought Cassie. It's not every day one has a brother return from the dead.

''Plenty for us all, Keir. Plenty for you and me and Mother and my crew. But we have to hurry,'' Paolo said, as if he had noticed Keir's indecision. ''I'm being blackmailed by a partner I didn't want in the first place. I've let him help me salvage. But now I'm going to leave him empty-handed.'' Paolo gave a bitter laugh.

The thought that had been eluding Cassie suddenly became clear. She knew exactly who Paolo's partner was. The huge, misshapen diver who hadn't followed her into the coral. The diver who wouldn't have entered the maze even if he had been small enough to slip through the tiny hole.

Suddenly a hand grabbed Cassie's arm and twisted it behind her.

''Well, well, what have we here?'' said a low voice in her ear. Cassie felt cold steel in the small of her back. She turned and looked into the glittering eyes of Todd Wrightson.

"*C*assandra!" said Keir, as Todd shoved her forward. "What are you doing here?"

"She's pretending to be a detective." Todd laughed menacingly.

"A detective?" Keir echoed.

"And not a very good one, in my opinion," continued Todd.

"I was good enough to uncover your smuggling operation, Todd," Cassie said. "Now the coast guard knows all about you."

"But you weren't good enough to keep from getting caught, were you?" Todd said in a taunting voice that was full of self-satisfaction. "And I'll be out of these waters before the coast guard ever catches up," he finished.

"Sure we will, Wrightson," said Paolo heartily. Cassie could see he was uneasy. "But let's get out of here. We can leave this girl tied up. We'll have plenty of time to get to Mexico before anyone finds her. If they ever do."

"But they won't, Paolo," said Keir, looking at his brother in disbelief. "You and I are the only ones who know about this cave. That's how I knew you were the one who had sent the note telling me to come here. If we leave Cassandra tied up, she'll die."

"Don't worry about it," said Paolo, keeping his eyes on Todd. "We'll let someone know about her in time."

"But—" Keir began.

"We?" asked Todd. "Who's this 'we'? You were going to leave without me, Paolo. Just you and your brother."

"Of course I wasn't, Wrightson," Paolo said, still trying to pretend everything was normal. "Sure, I was going to bring Keir in with us—"

"Now I'm going to leave without you," Todd continued smoothly, as if there had been no interruption. "I'll take your crew because I need them. But they'll go with me gladly. Loyalty doesn't seem to last long where gold is involved."

"You swine!" Paolo shouted. Pushing Cassie aside, he threw himself across the cave and jumped his former partner.

His hand on Todd's arm, Paolo tried to wrest the gun away from him. While they struggled, Keir pulled Cassie back against the cave wall.

A gunshot echoed in the small rock chamber. Then Paolo slumped to the floor.

"You've killed him!" Keir shouted, running to his brother.

"Everyone thought he was dead anyway," Todd said with a short laugh. He was still holding his gun.

Cassie ran over to Keir and knelt beside the wounded man. She felt for his pulse. "He's not dead, Keir," she said. "See, the bullet only grazed him." She pointed to an ugly bruise on Paolo's head.

"Too bad for him," Todd said grimly. "He won't last long, anyway. Now enough talk. I need to be on my way. The sooner I get to Mexico, the sooner I can relax."

"With all that gold," Cassie said reflectively. She stood up. "But the gold wasn't what you were really after, was it, Todd?" She knew that this smuggler had failed in his real quest.

"You want to rub it in, don't you, Cassandra?" Todd said softly. "But no, I don't care that much about the gold. Certainly not enough to steal it. But the only way to the jaguar was through Paolo, and Paolo wanted the gold."

"What's so special about the jaguar, Todd?" said

Cassie. She wanted to keep him talking as long as possible.

"The jaguar is one of the most perfect gold sculptures ever made by the hand of man," Todd said dreamily. "It is the prize of a lifetime, the bounty of kings."

"And you wanted it badly enough to spend extra time underwater, despite your phobia," said Cassie, recalling the unusual shape of the huge diver who had chased her with a spear gun. Todd's extra air tank had given him a monstrous appearance in the dark waters. "But if you had found the gold jaguar, what would you have done with it?"

"I would have hidden it away, where no one but me could see it," Todd said. His eyes were lit with a strange glow. "Just owning the statue would have made me happy for the rest of my life."

"You wanted to keep the statue hidden like your other artifacts, didn't you, Todd?" asked Cassie.

"You and your prying eyes," said Todd. "Oh, I was angry when I found you among my valuables." He frowned at the memory. "But I kept my temper. I already knew you were a detective, you see. I just wanted final confirmation."

"When did you find out?" asked Cassie. Keir had come to stand beside her, his arm thrown protectively around her shoulder.

"Oh, that first day, when you were checking through the damaged equipment," Todd said. "You mentioned to your friend that you thought someone knew you were a detective, and I overheard you. But after I talked to you at my party, I realized Paolo and I had better settle for the gold we had and get out while the getting was good. Before you stumbled onto the real reason for the vandalism."

"Slowing up Whit," said Keir.

"And keeping him from getting to Oyster Key," added Cassie. "That was why you destroyed the sonar and had Paolo steal the reading that was taken the day he supposedly drowned."

"Ah, yes, poor Paolo," Todd said sarcastically. "He was against the vandalism from the very start. He wanted to get as much gold as he could without hurting anyone." Todd turned to Keir. "You needn't have worried about his leaving Cassandra here to drown. He was much too softhearted for that."

"My brother—" Keir began.

"Your brother is a fool," Todd said roughly. "If he hadn't sent you that note today, we would have gotten away cleanly. He wouldn't be lying there half dead, and you and Cassandra wouldn't be here now. No, Paolo should never have tried to double-cross me. Now none of you will ever get out of here."

"What do you mean, we'll never get out of here, Todd?" Keir said indignantly. "What are you planning? Paolo's injured. He needs help soon."

"Well, I can't just leave you all here to follow me

or call the coast guard, now can I?" Todd said menacingly.

"How did you get hooked up with Paolo anyway, Todd?" asked Cassie, desperate to keep the conversation going. She had to think of a way out of this predicament. "You seem so different from each other."

"I ran into him in Miami, right after he 'died,' " Todd explained. "He found the gold on the bottom of the ocean the day of the storm, and when he couldn't make it back to the ship, he saved himself by swimming to the nearest reef. A boat picked him up the next day and took him to Miami."

"I always knew Paolo was too good a swimmer to drown like that," muttered Keir.

"When I met him he was trying to buy a boat with the few gold bars he had been able to carry from the wreck," continued Todd. "I got the whole story and forced him into taking me on as a partner."

"You blackmailed him, didn't you?" asked Cassie. "You told him that if he wouldn't share the treasure, you'd turn him in. You even talked him out of buying a new boat." Another piece of the puzzle fell into place for her. "You just painted and disguised Whit's boat after you stole it."

"Good thinking, Cassandra," Todd said approvingly. "Maybe you're not such an amateur after all. I wanted to save the money. It was the only mistake I've made," he admitted. "By the time we overhauled that old boat, we'd spent almost as much as a new boat would have cost."

"But you had to do it right," Cassie went on. "You didn't have time for a boat that would break down."

"That's true," Todd said. "Paolo stayed in Miami to disguise the *Sea Adventurer*. It gave him time to dye his hair and start growing a beard."

"After you got away with stealing a ship, the other vandalism must have seemed easy," Cassie mused. How were she and Keir going to get out of this cave?

"Don't you know that changing a ship's name is bad luck, Todd?" said Keir.

Todd laughed. "I haven't found that to be true. Turn around, Keir. I brought only enough rope for two. I hope it will stretch to accommodate three."

Keeping Keir between himself and Cassie, Todd managed to tie Keir's wrists while still holding the gun on him. Then he sat Keir down and tied Paolo's hands with the short end of the same rope.

"Your turn, Cassie." He motioned for Cassie to sit on the other side of Keir. What choice did she have?

"There's just one thing I want to know, Todd," said Cassie. "Who kept trying to scare me away, you or Paolo?" She already knew the answer, but she had to keep him talking.

"Oh, I did, of course," said Todd. "You don't

scare easily, I'll say that for you. That leaking air tank was just a happy accident. But then I resorted to that ridiculous chicken, hoping you'd blame Keir or that crazy mother of his. I even left you the note. You can't say I didn't warn you."

"But you didn't throw me over the side of the *Sea Hawk*," Cassie retorted. "Paolo did."

"That's right," Todd replied. "Paolo was panicked and didn't know what to do. If it had been me, you'd never have left that boat. Just the way you're never going to leave this cave."

Todd shoved Cassie down beside Keir. She felt the rope bite into her wrists. She tried to keep them slightly apart, but Todd noticed and twisted the rope even tighter. Then he brought the rope down around her legs and bound them, too. He still had enough rope for Keir's legs, but had run out by the time he got to Paolo.

"No more rope," Todd said. "Well, he's in no condition to get up and walk anyhow."

That done, Todd bundled the remaining gold into his jacket and clumsily swung it over his shoulders.

"I'm afraid I've got to go now," he said, turning around to look at his captives for the last time. "As the saying goes, time and tide wait for no man. Or woman either, Cassandra." He gave them a small, tight smile and staggered out of the cave.

"What did he mean by that?" asked Cassie.

"You'll find out," said Keir miserably. "I can't tell you how sorry I am about all this, Cassandra."

"It's not your fault, Keir," Cassie said consolingly. She had been awfully glad to discover that Keir was innocent.

"It's all because of my brother, though," said Keir.

"You're not responsible for your brother's actions," Cassie said gently. "And you've had to suffer all this time, thinking he was dead."

"My poor mother," said Keir, sighing.

"Where was your mother tonight, Keir?" asked Cassie. "When you went to find her, she wasn't in her room."

"Yes, I wanted to show her Paolo's note telling me to meet him at the cave," said Keir. "But I guess she got up and went for a walk on the beach. She often does that when she can't sleep. We'd spent the day together going through Paolo's old things, so she must have been upset."

"I can see why," said Cassie. Now she knew what Keir's "personal business" had been.

"How did your necklace get on board the *Anhinga*, Keir?" asked Cassie, changing the subject. She was still putting the pieces of the puzzle together while she thought about how to escape from their predicament.

"I got a note asking me to go there," answered Keir. "The message said there was something about Paolo that I should know. But as soon as I stepped on board, someone hit me over the head. By the time I came to, the sonar was smashed. I was afraid Whit would think I did it, so I took off." Keir sighed. "I guess that was pretty stupid. But I was too confused to think properly. Then the next day when Whit questioned me, I was so angry that someone would use my dead brother to play a trick on me, I just couldn't talk about it."

"And you didn't realize immediately that your doubloon was gone?" asked Cassie.

"No, I didn't miss it till later." Keir shook his head. "Now I know that Todd must have left it there to throw suspicion on me. He must have really hated me, to set me up that way."

Todd Wrightson has a strange, twisted personality, Cassie mused. He is so intelligent, so knowledgeable in his field. Yet his obsession for rare objects pushed him over the edge. In the end, his objects totally possessed him.

Suddenly Cassie realized her feet were getting wet. Looking down, she saw water swirling around her ankles.

"Keir, there's water in here," she said. She could hear the panic in her voice. "The ocean is right up to my feet!"

"I'm sorry, Cassandra. I'm really sorry," Keir apologized again.

"Stop saying you're sorry. What's happening?" Cassie was desperately afraid she knew.

"The tide is coming in," Keir said reluctantly. "At high tide, this cave is totally submerged. It's only a matter of time before we drown."

*T*ime and tide wait for no man. Cassie remembered Todd Wrightson's parting words. Now she knew what he meant.

She struggled with the ropes that bound her. "How long will it take for the water to flood the cave?" she asked, fear in her voice.

"I don't know what time high tide is," said Keir. "But since the water is already inside the cave, I'd say in about two hours."

Then they had perhaps an hour. They would have had longer if they were standing up, but since they were sitting the water would be above their heads long before the cave was completely full.

"Is Paolo still unconscious?" asked Cassie.

"Let me check," Keir said. He bent over his wounded brother. "Paolo, can you hear me?"

Paulo moaned in response. "Keir, what—"

"He's coming around," said Keir.

"Tell him to hold on," said Cassie. "I'll think of a way to get us out of here."

Cassie pulled and tugged on the rope until her wrists started to feel raw. As the salt water splashed around them, the salt made the abrasions sting and burn. If the rope got completely wet, would it shrink and make the knots tighter?

"We've all got to move, Keir," said Cassie. "Even if we have to drag Paolo. If I can get over to the cave wall, maybe I can find a sharp edge of a rock to cut the rope against."

"Okay, we'll all push together with our feet. You too, Paolo," Keir instructed. "It's our only chance to get out of here."

Keir and Cassie wriggled backward, pushing at the now muddy floor with their feet, while Paolo dragged himself along. Cassie despaired at how little they seemed to move with each effort. It seemed to take them hours just to get close to the cave wall. By then the water was swirling around their waists and splashing onto their faces.

Facing the wall, Cassie felt along the rough surface until she found an edge that jutted out sharply from the surrounding rock. Lifting their arms together, she and Keir rubbed the rope against the rock. Each movement on their part brought a groan from Paolo.

"I'm drowning—drowning," said Paolo. He was finding it difficult to support himself above the swelling water. "I have to save the gold. Look Mama, look at the gold. It's yours, all yours."

"He's delirious," said Keir, with a catch in his voice. "Oh, Paolo, what have you done? I always thought you were so smart."

They kept moving the rope back and forth across the rock. The water swirled around Cassie's chest and splashed onto her chin as it crashed in and out of the cave. The waves extinguished the light from Paolo's torch. Luckily, by this time dawn was breaking so Cassie could still see what she was doing.

It wasn't the rubbing that finally released the rope. With a desperate tug, Cassie caught the rope on the rock outcropping and threw herself forward. With a final snap, the rope broke. She fell face down into the cool ocean.

"I'm free, Keir," Cassie said. She untied his hands, then bent to untie her legs. It was difficult under the water, but she finally released them. Then they both worked to free Paolo.

Feeling as though she'd just fought an all-out war, Cassie took a deep breath and willed herself to find the strength to get out of this cave.

"This way, Cassandra," said Keir, pointing to the rear of the cave. "Help me with Paolo."

"But that's the entrance," objected Cassie, looking in the opposite direction.

"The cave goes all the way through," explained Keir. "The mouth isn't as obvious on the cove side. In fact, we'll have to dive to get out that way. But it will be easier to tow Paolo through the water than carry him through the mangrove swamp."

Cassie had a sudden thought. "When we come out of the cave into the cove, we'll be on Treasure Beach, won't we, Keir?" she asked. When he nodded, she went on, "And you used this cave when you 'disappeared' that day you scared me and Alex!"

"So the ace detective finally figures it out," said Keir, with the ghost of his old teasing grin.

They sloshed through the water to the back of the cave, supporting Paolo between them. When the cave ceiling dropped down almost to the level of the water, they knew they had to dive.

"Just swim straight ahead about thirty feet," instructed Keir. "You go first. I'll follow with Paolo."

Kicking off her tennis shoes, Cassie forced herself to stop thinking. She took several deep breaths and then dived into the murky water. She glided on and on, swimming as hard as she could. When she thought her lungs would surely burst, she surfaced, holding one arm above her in case she had misjudged the distance.

She came out into the calm water of the cove. Tossing her hair behind her, she breathed the sweet early morning air. The ordeal was over.

Keir surfaced beside her with Paolo on his back. The wounded man was still conscious and had clung to his younger brother during the long underwater dive.

"Swim the rest of the way in," Keir told her, panting from exhaustion. "We're going to take it slowly."

Cassie knew that she was as tired as she'd ever been in her life. But being free gave her a burst of energy. She breaststroked toward the line of beach glimmering faintly in the dawn. In no time, she bumped her knees on the sand and stumbled out onto Treasure Beach.

She lay a long time on the beach, trying to catch her breath. She was dimly aware that Keir and Paolo had crawled out of the surf, and were lying a little distance away. Finally, when she was feeling a little stronger, she called out, "Okay, let's go."

Together she and Keir supported Paolo down the beach and up the shell path that led to Owena's. Keir called out to his mother as soon as they entered the big house.

"Mama, look who's here. Mama!"

"She's probably in the kitchen, Keir," suggested Cassie.

As soon as Fidelia saw them, Cassie knew they should have prepared her for the shock of seeing Paolo.

Staring at her "dead" son with her intense dark

eyes, Fidelia sat absolutely still. Then she put down her coffee cup and started to moan loudly.

"The spirits of the dead have come into this house. I knew it would happen. I saw it in my dreams." Covering her face, Fidelia started to rock back and forth in her seat.

"It's all right, Mama," Keir said, kneeling by her side. "It's really Paolo and he's not dead." He motioned to his brother to come over. "See, he's real."

Fidelia took Paolo's head in her hands and burst into tears.

Awakened by Fidelia's moaning, Owena and Alex burst into the kitchen.

"Paolo!" Owena cried out. "Cassandra! What's going on?"

"You're wet," Alex said. "Have you been outside?"

Cassie settled herself into one of the kitchen chairs. "It'll take a long time to tell you the whole story," she said wearily. "But first we have to get Paolo to the hospital. And then I have to call the coast guard."

Owena took charge of the situation at once. "Certainly, Cassandra. Our short-wave radio is in the office. Come with me." Cassie followed her to the back of the house.

Owena called for a medical crew and helicopter, then turned the radio over to Cassie.

"Coast guard, this is Cassandra Best on Sand Dollar Key. This is an emergency. The ship *Sea Hawk*, out of Key West, is heading for Mexico with a cargo of smuggled gold. The captain is Todd Wrightson. He should be booked for smuggling and assault." Cassie gave the officer in charge as much information as she could and then signed off.

Leaning back in her chair, Cassie sighed in relief. She could relax now that the coast guard was on Todd's trail.

"You must get out of those wet clothes," suggested Owena. "I'll find some bandages for your wrists while you take a hot shower."

But before Cassie could leave the office, a familiar voice came over the short wave.

"*Anhinga* calling Sand Dollar Key. Owena, come in. Can you hear me?"

"It's Whit," said Owena. "Answer him, Cassandra."

"*Anhinga*, this is Cassandra Best. Come in, Whit."

"Cassandra, is that you? Is Owena there?"

"Yes, we're both here. I have so much to tell you—" said Cassie.

"I have so much to tell *you*, Cassandra," said Whit. "Something wonderful has happened. Are you both sitting down? I've finally found it—the *Madreperla*!"

"**Y**ou've found the treasure? Oh, Whit, tell us the whole story," exclaimed Cassie. She was thrilled by the news. Clutching Cassie's shoulder, Owena sat down to listen.

"After what you told me, Cassandra, I couldn't sleep last night," Whit began. "So I roused the crew and we set out to find Oyster Key as soon as the rain stopped. Between your directions, my intuition, and just a little bit of luck, it took us no time at all to find the site." Whit gave an incredulous laugh. "We hit on the *Madreperla* just a few minutes ago. I wanted the two of you to be the first to know."

Owena took the microphone and said, "What about the jaguar, Whit? Have you found it?"

"Not yet, Owena," Whit replied. "But it's only a

matter of time now. I'll have it for the foundation party. I promise."

Whit kept his promise. On the night of the party, hundreds of guests buzzed with excitement as they filed past the treasures displayed in the foyer of Owena's home.

"I've never seen anything like it," Cassie exclaimed, pointing at the statue of the golden jaguar. It was so lifelike that it looked as if it might leap right off its perch. In the glare of the spotlights, its emerald collar glittered like stars. Two huge emerald eyes stared at her defiantly. The jaguar was so beautiful she could almost understand why Todd had risked his career for it.

"Do you think Todd will be able to see it before he goes to jail?" asked Alex.

"It seems only fair, since the search for it has ruined his life," Cassie said. She felt she could have a little sympathy for Todd now that Paolo was recovering and Todd and his crew were behind bars.

Sipping a glass of punch, Cassie wandered outside into the soft Southern evening. She marveled at the way the pool had been transformed by a shimmering fleet of floating candles. Colorful flowers drifted among the candle boats, and hundreds of lanterns flickered along the garden paths.

Dancing had started at dusk on the terrace. The guests mingled by the candle-lit tables set up on one

side of the pool and talked about diving for treasure. Whit's discovery of the *Madreperla* overshadowed the rumors of vandalism that had preceded it. Cassie was glad that Whit was the center of attention tonight.

After dancing and conversation, the guests sampled the fresh lobster that had been flown in from Miami and the extraordinary Key lime pie that was Fidelia's specialty.

"Owena sure knows how to throw a party, doesn't she?" Whit said, coming up to Cassie as she watched the dancers spin past. "And Fidelia's catering is better than ever."

"It's splendid," agreed Cassie. "Fidelia has apologized for her rudeness to me. I'm sure it was only because of her fear that Keir would be hurt just like Paolo was if the expedition continued."

"I guess another apology is in order," said Whit. "As you know, at first I had my doubts about your detective abilities, Cassandra."

"No apology needed, Whit. I'm just glad I could help."

"I feel on top of the world tonight," Whit said. "Maybe it's time for me to retire."

"Until another challenge comes your way? Another sunken treasure, perhaps?" Cassie smiled.

Whit laughed. "You're a pretty good judge of character, Miss Best."

They watched Owena float across the dance floor

with one of the divers from Whit's crew. Alex waltzed by with Keir.

"A gentleman would ask you to dance," said Whit, holding out his hand. "But first, I want you to have this token of my appreciation." He pulled a small box out of his pocket.

Cassie took the box and opened it. Inside was a beautiful gold chain that held a gleaming gold doubloon. "Oh, Whit, it's lovely."

"It's the first gold coin from the *Madreperla*, Cassandra," Whit said, beaming.

"I'll treasure it. Thank you." Cassie slipped the chain around her neck.

Keir cut in on their conversation. "Give the younger guys a chance, Whit," he said. Whit gave Cassie a smile and left to find Owena.

"You look much better without all that seaweed in your hair, Cassandra," said Keir, grinning.

"I see you've recovered your sense of humor," returned Cassie. They laughed together.

"Paolo is going to be all right." Keir's smile lit up his face. "He'll have to spend some time in prison, but at least he's alive."

"Maybe by the time he's out, he'll be cured of gold fever," said Cassie.

"You saved our lives, Cassandra," said Keir. "You're a very special person and a great detective."

* * *

Alex had to remind Cassie to hurry or she'd miss her flight home. Owena, Alex, and Cassie had stopped by the foundation to buy Melanie a silver coin for her charm bracelet. Cassie knew that her purchase would help finance more treasure hunts.

On the way out of the gift shop, they stopped by the gallery where the golden jaguar was now on display. Cassie wanted to see the statue one last time.

"How can I ever thank you, Cassandra?" said Owena warmly. "Without you, this whole expedition would have crumbled. And worse, this very important artifact might have found its way into the wrong hands."

"Thank you for believing in me," Cassie replied. "This case turned out to be more complicated than I first thought. I'm glad I was able to solve it."

"I never doubted that you would," Owena said. She hugged Cassie and the three left for the airport.

"I'm going to miss you, Cassandra," said Alex as they waited in the terminal. "You're the 'best'!"

"I'll miss you terribly, too," Cassie said. She hugged Alex one more time and ran to board her plane.

"I'll be calling," Alex shouted after her.

Cassie was looking out of her window when the plane took off and flew over the wide blue ocean before circling north to Miami. Another case had been solved.

* * *

Before she knew it, the big jet was roaring down the runway at the Milltown airport.

"You're not as tan as I thought you'd be," said Melanie, the minute she saw her sister in the waiting area.

"Oh, there's more to do in Florida than lie in the sun," said Cassie, winking at Gran.

"Like what?" Melanie asked, as they walked to the parking lot to find the car.

"Oh, like shopping and boating and scuba diving," Cassie said vaguely. And like uncovering a smuggling ring and finding golden treasure, she added to herself. But she'd have to tell Gran that part later.

Already Key West seemed like another world. Her treasure-hunting adventure was behind her.

And Cassandra Best, detective, could hardly wait for her next case.

The Cassandra Mysteries